THE ABSOLUTION OF JONAH BANE

THE BANES OF LAKE'S CROSSING

R.L. MERRILL

CELIE BAY PUBLICATIONS LLC

PRAISE FOR THE BANES OF LAKE'S CROSSING

"Each installment of this compilation will tantalize and terrify you. An absolute must read!"

— ~ KERRIGAN BYRNE - INTERNATIONAL BESTSELLING AUTHOR OF THE VICTORIAN REBELS SERIES

"The story was fresh, funny, sexy, and a bit horrifying (in the best possible way). I loved being both in the past and the present, and I am excited for what these ladies will write in the future!"

— ~ K.G.A. ON AMAZON

"Together, these three authors have created interconnecting stories that are both chilling, and full of suspense."

— ~ LOVES TO READ ON AMAZON

.

PRAISE FOR R.L. MERRILL

Connection - Gifted Book Two

"A fast-paced and fun fusion of supernatural romance and mainstream thriller."

~Kirkus Reviews

"An ever-present element of suspense reinforces the story's rapid pace, and Merrill delivers a riveting conclusion that will entice readers with the possibility of future installments."

— ~BOOKLIFE REVIEWS

Brains and Brawn - Summer of Hush Book Two

"Merrill does a wonderful job creating an expansive yet strong set of supporting characters, who are each well-rounded and vital to the overall narrative."

— ~BOOKLIFE REVIEWS

World Created by Ellay Branton, Kimberlie L. Faye, and R.L. Merrill

Edited by Kelli Collins - Edit Me This

Cover by Yosbe Design

❀ Created with Vellum

For those running from their pasts, may you find peace and absolution, and the family you deserve...Love is Love

FROM THE BANES OF LAKE'S CROSSING - ORIGINS

INTRODUCTION

The biggest little city in the world was founded on a lie. The legends tell us that the city called Reno, Nevada was founded as a gambling haven for those who had been mining silver and later it became the divorce capital of the United States. But the ominous story goes deeper than that. It goes as deep as the lines from which that silver came.

In 1860, four brothers tunneled beneath the surface, looking to find the next Comstock Lode. They left their families behind in search of the valuable metals being brought forth from the Earth in order to do the Lord's work. Their plan was to settle down near Virginia City and build a new church to save the souls of those seeking riches.

Lionel, William, Nathaniel, and Jonah Call went below ground on a chilly fall morning in 1860 and were never seen again. The official story was an explosion caused their brace work to collapse, trapping them all inside. Word reached their families a month later, and services were held to bless their souls and send them into the afterlife.

In 1861, Myron Lake purchased a primitive log-constructed settlement and bridge crossing the Truckee River, and within months turned it into a profitable business, receiving a toll permit for the bridge, which he quickly reconstructed to be able to withstand the frequent flooding at that portion of the river. Lake received capital with which to complete these projects from investors, who remained anonymous for decades. No one was quite sure how Lake managed to run so many successful businesses in the area, but there were rumors, especially about his four investors.

Legend has it that four men went down into the Earth as good, solid Christian men—and returned as something much more sinister.

1

Present Day Fort Bragg, CA

"That guy over at the inn said you could help me."

Byron could kick himself. *WTF, bruh, where's your game?*

He'd had the most confusing conversation with the man named Joe Bane last night about his family history, and he'd followed Bane's directions to come speak to this woman Darcy, but the rest of his visit to Fort Bragg was kind of fuzzy, as if he'd had too much to drink. He'd come here to confront Joe Bane about a family quarrel concerning a brooch bouquet and whether or not Bane's ancestors had stolen from the Manwarings, but he had more questions now that he was face to face with this beautiful woman.

Darcy smiled. "I guess you mean Mr. Bane." She cocked out a hip and crossed her arms over her chest. She wore a short black skater dress that hit her high on the thigh and her long black hair was gathered in two pigtails at her shoulders. Byron was mesmerized by the combination of electric purple lipstick, white teeth and a pink tongue when she spoke. Her body language was closed off, but she had a hint of amusement in her eerie green eyes.

Her eyes.

There was something familiar about them.

Byron smirked. "I guess I do. He told me you could help me with this," he said, holding out his phone. He'd taken a picture of the brooch bouquet before he left in case this Bane dude was old and forgetful. Turned out the man was nothing like what he'd expected, but he couldn't remember much of the night before. Whatever was in that wine he'd given Byron had fucked him up good.

Darcy's eyebrows nearly met in the middle as she frowned at the image. She used her fingers to zoom in and Byron couldn't help but notice how long they were. And slim. Dainty. Her nails were painted an electric purple to match her lipstick. Damn, but her lips were calling for all of Byron's attention.

"And Mr. Bane said I could make this?"

"He did. He, uh, won't give me back the original, but he said you could make a duplicate." *Why couldn't he give it to me?* Every time Byron tried to remember, his thoughts became murkier.

"I can certainly try," she said as she tapped some buttons on his phone. "When do you need it?"

"My little sister is getting married in a couple of months. She and my mom and grandma are all hollerin' for me to get this bouquet, so..."

"So I better get this made for you," she said with a smirk. "It shouldn't take me terribly long. I'll have to see how much silver I have, and I'll have to order the pearls to match those."

"You can really make this?"

Darcy's eyes bugged out and Byron was quick to backpedal. "I don't mean any disrespect. It just seems like a lot of work."

She shrugged. "I've made all kinds of things. I learned from my parents," she said, handing back his phone. "I texted the picture to myself so you have my number."

Byron couldn't stop staring at her as she pulled out her phone and gazed at the photo. Lines of concentration formed on her forehead as she zoomed in on certain areas of the picture.

The bouquet itself was made up of about twenty brooches attached to wires that gathered into a base and then the base was wrapped with ribbon.

"I don't know if I can get the ribbon to look as authentic as this."

"Oh, whatever you can do. Maybe I can just say it fell apart and I got some new ribbon."

Darcy grinned and shook her head. "You really don't know women, do you?"

Byron blanched at her accusation. "I was raised by my mama and grandma and I have three little sisters. My whole life has been women. I think I know them pretty damn well."

Darcy came around the corner of the counter and closed the distance between them. He backed up a step when she wedged herself between him and the counter, and then hopped up on it to sit in front of him.

"Right. Well. I'll do the very best I can to match everything." She swung her feet a bit which brought Byron's attention to her shapely thighs. The muscles beneath her skin flexed as she moved and damn, did it do something to his insides.

"You have any pictures of stuff you've made?"

"Why? You don't trust me?"

He was fucking this up six ways to Sunday.

"No! It's not that, I just, I don't want to get my ass handed to me when I get home and this thing isn't right."

Darcy looked over her shoulder at the clock on the wall. It was one of those black cat ones that the eyes moved back and forth and the tail wagged below it. Byron looked around and realized there was a helluva lot of black cat themed shit in the store.

"I get off at four. Why don't you come back and I'll take you over to my workshop, then you can see I'm the real deal."

Byron had been planning to hit the road for home, but why? He had nothing to go back to except nagging women and more disappointments. Besides, he wanted more answers from Bane. How the hell could he be the same guy who bought the inn from the auction when Byron's grandfather lost it back in the sixties? He didn't look any older than maybe late twenties early thirties. And some story about the silver—did he say the guy's name was Bane? Byron was so confused. He wanted answers. And he wanted the bouquet. And he wanted a job. And he wanted to spend more time with the gorgeous Darcy.

All of those wants pointed to him staying in town.

"I'll be waiting for you."

Darcy gave him a knowing smile.

.

2

_____

P resent Day Fort Bragg, CA

JONAH WATCHED as Byron left the shop. From his room at the top of the water tower next to the inn, he could see most of his end of town. He watched as Byron went out to his Jeep, started the car and then turned it off. He got out and walked down the street, pausing to look back in the direction of the inn before heading down Main Street.

He'd met with Darcy. Jonah questioned the wisdom of putting those two together, but what was done was done. He hated the position Byron was in and hated the hand he'd had in the drama in which the Manwaring family was embroiled.

No, he hadn't gone to San Francisco on business, but Jonah needed some space from the young man who looked so much like his grandfather. He hoped the younger Byron had less of an impulsive nature than the man he was named after, but knew it was likely to be true.

Jonah sat in his favorite chair in his small room and stared out at the ocean. Memories assaulted him from all angles. All he'd lost. All he'd fought against. The evil inside him had been at rest for the past decade, and it took less and less to sustain him these days, but something stirred in him when Byron crossed the threshold of his home looking for answers. And he'd wanted to give them. For some damn reason, Jonah wanted to unload the whole sordid tale, who knows, perhaps gain absolution for the sins of his past. But then as Byron got more and more intoxicated off of the tainted wine, Jonah began to question his judgment. He'd been alive for over one hundred and seventy years with no sign he was going anywhere. Was he really stupid enough to reveal himself and his curse to this young man who already had enough on his plate, just to ease his own conscience?

But Byron was just as affected by the curse Jonah had carried these long years. He just didn't know it yet.

His cell phone rang and he stared at it. The ring was Darth Vader's march. Darcy. She'd set it up on his phone, and he didn't know how to turn it off.

"Yes, darling," he answered sarcastically.

"Why did you send him to me?"

Jonah stretched out his long legs and took a long pull on his scotch. "Because he needs the bouquet. You're the most brilliant silversmith I know."

"Bullshit," she said with a laugh. "*You're* the most brilliant silversmith you know."

Jonah chuckled. Darcy always could make him smile. He was incredibly proud of her. "Regardless, he needs the bouquet, you can make it for him. What else did he say?"

"He's a very confused young man. Did you give him the wine last night?"

She knew all his secrets. "I did. But then I said too much, so I gave him more. When will you see him again?"

It was quiet for too long on the other end of the line. "He's coming after work. He wanted to see what I can do."

A feeling of powerlessness descended upon Jonah. He'd set this in motion the moment he agreed to see Byron. He'd kept such a tight leash on everything for so long, why now would he bring someone in who could end it all?

Perhaps he wanted it to end. The years had been long and unforgiving. He'd done all the good he could to counteract the evil the cursed silver brought into the world, but it never seemed to be enough.

"Just be careful," Jonah warned.

"Careful? For myself or for his sake?"

Too damned smart.

"Both."

3

F ort Bragg, CA 1929

JIMMY MANWARING PLAYED piano nightly at the Golden West Saloon. He accepted payment in alcohol. He never spoke, and no one knew much about him except that he'd been playing piano every night for about the past eight years. Hope often made up stories in her head about him, sharing them with the other ladies that lived in the dormitory late at night. They'd giggle and laugh as though they didn't have a care in the world, when in reality it seemed to be the furthest from the truth for them all.

Hope Johnson served up drinks and food to the loggers who came in every weekend from the woods to spend their cash on women and, if they were lucky, bootlegged liquor. The Golden West Saloon had both a' plenty, and so did the hundred or so bars in Fort Bragg at that time. Hope was happy with the anonymity here and prayed it would continue once the babies were born. She and another runaway named Bonnie Collins had found each other on the train from

Missouri and both hoped California would be different. Someone at the train station in Sacramento told them that they were always looking for women to cook and serve food up on the Mendocino Coast and in the town of Fort Bragg, so they'd taken the train to the end of the line. That was four months ago. Hope couldn't keep her secret much longer.

Her back ached and her feet were swollen in her shoes, but she and Bonnie worked their shifts and planned to take turns working when the twins came. The doctor she'd seen in San Francisco had been sure she was having twins. She'd been sick, sore, and emotionally wrecked after the awful trip and had fallen into Bonnie's arms, weeping and afraid.

"Don't worry," Bonnie had said, patting her head. "We'll be fine. We'll raise them babies together."

Both women had been on the run, and it was fate that brought them together on a train platform in St. Louis that dark and stormy winter's night. Hope had stolen enough cash from her husband's stash that she was sure she could get to California but knew it wouldn't last forever. Bonnie had been promised to a man much older and refused to marry him, so she'd run off with nothing and planned to figure it all out once she boarded a train. Hope needed Bonnie as her cover, Bonnie needed Hope's money. Their bond formed during that trip would last a lifetime.

But this night Hope watched Jimmy even more closely than usual. His music was different. It was ominous, foreboding, not the usual uplifting ragtime that the guests expected to hear from him. Charlie, the owner of the saloon, frowned so deeply his bushy eyebrows nearly met his bushier mustache.

"Hope. Go tell that sonofabitch to change his tune before I throw him outta here. Can't have that doom and gloom playing when these men are thinking about getting amorous! It's bad for business!"

"But Charlie, he never speaks. Does he even talk? What if—"

"I don't pay you to ask questions, young lady. If you want to keep your job, you'll do as I say."

He threw a towel at her and went back to pouring drinks,

watching her with an angry set to his jaw. Hope knew better than to push her luck. He'd slapped her more than once for questioning his orders, and she just couldn't have that. She had the babies to think about. She just hoped she could keep her growing bump hidden for a few more weeks.

Hope wiped her hands on the towel nervously as she approached the big man now pounding on the keys. She didn't recognize the tune. It sounded really old.

"Mr. Manwaring? Um, Charlie says—"

"I don't give a damn what that fool says."

Hope was startled to hear his voice. He apparently could speak.

"Please, sir. I can't lose my job. Can you—"

Jimmy turned to glare at her but his glance softened. And then he looked at her growing belly. Hope panicked. *Could he tell?*

"This is no place for you," he growled, but then he started playing an upbeat boogie-woogie tune that had every head in the joint turned his way. A hush fell over the crowd as this white man played "negro music" like he was born to do it. His left hand played the bass line and his right fluttered over the keys at an almost inhuman speed.

Hope realized she'd been holding her breath and took a few steps back from the piano, but Jimmy's eyes never left her.

"Why is he looking at you like that?" Bonnie asked her as she was passing with a bin full of dirty dishes to carry to the back.

"I have no idea," Hope answered, but then she felt something. Her babies! They were moving! She was somewhere between four and five months along now, if she counted the time correctly, and she hadn't sat still long enough to feel anything. Something about this music, however, must have called to her unborn children. Her hand absently stroked her midsection and she smiled at Jimmy, but he immediately shook his head and glanced over his shoulder at the bar where Charlie was still frowning.

Hope cursed to herself and hurried back to the kitchen. When Bonnie returned, she told her what had happened. The two women embraced and then went back to work, only allowing themselves a brief moment to share in the joy that was about to enter their lives.

Every night afterward, Hope made a point to stand as near to the piano as she could without calling attention to herself in hopes that Jimmy's music would awaken her children. In her dreary life in this place where the sun rarely shined, the babies were all she dreamed about. In those dreams, she and Bonnie were living in a cottage somewhere, Hope caring for the children and cooking, maybe looking after some chickens, gardening, raising food for them to eat, and Bonnie could work in a kitchen somewhere other than the saloon where she was constantly fighting off the attentions of the men. She was a beautiful redheaded woman with pale skin. Hope's dark skin often brought negative attention, but things hadn't been as bad as she thought they might be. Here in Fort Bragg where Black folk were few in numbers, she didn't blend. She worried often about her children and what kind of life they would have here, but she just couldn't think that far ahead.

Jimmy never looked at her that way. The white man always kept an eye on her, ever since that first night, and she wondered what he thought about when he looked at her. Did he hate her? Did he even care what happened to her? Something in his eyes said he, too, understood what it meant to be different, to be *other* in this place.

A MONTH OR SO LATER, Hope was no longer able to hide her pregnancy. Bonnie had tried to adjust her dress, make the waist higher and the skirts fuller, but it was painfully obvious. She'd become adept at always carrying something in front of her to try to camouflage her growing belly, but she'd run out of time. She was only seven months pregnant. How much bigger was she going to get?

On a brisk fall night in mid-October, the saloon was especially crowded. News had spread that the financial world was having troubles, and the men were all gossiping about how it would impact the mill. Would the owners be affected?

"Woman, bring me another drink," a man said, slapping her hard on the bottom. She was so shocked, she dropped the bin she was carrying. Dishes and glass mugs crashed to the floor and the room went silent.

Hope immediately looked to Jimmy, who had stopped playing and rushed over to help her clean up the mess.

"No, don't stop playing," she whispered harshly to him. "Charlie will notice—"

"What in the hell is going on out there? Hope! Them dishes are coming out of your pay," Charlie yelled.

"Yes, sir," she replied, shooing Jimmy back to the piano. "Don't stop," she said once more.

Jimmy sat at the piano and began playing a sweet melody that reminded Hope of a lullaby. She smiled to herself as she finished placing the big pieces in the bin, and then Bonnie was by her side with a broom and a dustpan.

"Are you alright?" she whispered and Hope nodded, squeezing the hand Bonnie offered her. She had no idea what she would do without this woman who had become so close to her, who took such good care of her in her condition.

"Hope! Get over here," Charlie yelled.

She traded worried looks with Bonnie and carried her bin over to the bar.

"I want to see you in back," he said, grabbing her arm as he passed her by.

The moment she feared the most had arrived. She was in a state of panic, frightened of her volatile boss. She dragged her feet, wanting nothing to do with whatever he had to say to her, but she couldn't just leave. She and Bonnie needed this money if they were going to care for her twins.

Charlie pushed through the backdoor, into the alley and turned to face her. She hesitated in the doorway, not wanting that door closed in case he was really in a state.

"Why the hell didn't you tell me you were pregnant? Where is the father?"

"It's none of your business, Charlie," she said, angry to be put in this position. She'd left one abusive man to go to work for another and it just wasn't right. "I've done nothing wrong and it hasn't affected my work.

Charlie stepped forward and grabbed her arm hard. "I ain't having no little bastards running around here. Can't you do something about it?"

Hope tried to pull away, but Charlie's grip was strong.

"I plan on being gone by the time I have them."

Charlie laughed, and the sound made goosebumps break out on Hope's flesh. It was almost as though he were coming unhinged. Before she knew what he was about to do, he backhanded her so hard she dropped the bin of dishes, stumbled to the side, and fell against the wall.

"You get rid of it or I'll do it for you."

He raised up a fist to hit her again and Hope saw her life flash before her eyes. But then he stilled and his eyes grew wide as he stared at something behind her. She turned her head to see the hulking form of Jimmy Manwaring in the doorway, his fists clenched at his side.

"You touch her again and you will cease to breathe."

Charlie paused for a moment, his lips splitting into a grotesque smile and then he threw her to the ground. Hope tried to catch herself, but her head connected with the side of the building. Everything went black as she fell to the ground.

The last thing she remembered was Jimmy grabbing Charlie by the throat and tossing him like dirty laundry across the alley, his body slamming against the brick wall and landing with an ominous thud on the ground.

4

J immy knew he had only a short time to clean up his mess before someone called the constable. He spat in the direction of Charlie's corpse and growled as he thought about what he'd heard just moments before he'd made good on his promise to end the bartender's life.

"Hope!"

Bonnie must have followed them out. She ran to her friend and held her bloodied face in her hands.

"Oh my God, Hope! Hope, wake up," she pleaded, tears streaming down her face.

Jimmy approached them, and Bonnie moved to protect the unconscious woman like a mama bear.

"Don't you touch her," she growled, her hands already formed in claws. "You get away from her."

"I'm not going to hurt her," Jimmy said softly, his hands outstretched. "But we have to get her out of here before someone comes."

Hope began to stir and she stared up at Jimmy with frightened eyes.

"Hope," Bonnie said. "Baby, are you okay?"

Hope nodded, and started to stand, sucking in a breath. Her hands clutched her belly and she moaned. Bonnie whispered to her and helped her to stand on shaky legs.

"Take her to the Weller House. Go to the back entrance. Tell Pierre that I sent you."

"The Weller House? Why?" Bonnie asked.

"Never mind, just go and let me take care of this. Go!"

Bonnie pulled Hope's arm over her shoulder and led her as quick as possible from the alley. Once they were out of sight, Jimmy stormed over to Charlie's body and hefted the stout man over his shoulder. He didn't make a sound.

Charlie wasn't the first man Jimmy had killed, but his heart clenched at the thought that he'd further damned himself with this latest act.

He carried Charlie's body the mile walk from the saloon to the bluffs overlooking the ocean. With any luck, his fat body would sink or get stuck under the rocks and no one would find him. He could always burn the body, but a fire that size would be noticeable. Best to just dispose of him in the ocean.

Once he reached the cliffs, a lone seagull's cry echoed through the night sky. Odd for the bird to be out at this late hour. The waves crashing along the bluffs made a moaning sound and the bellowing horn from the Point Cabrillo Lighthouse crafted an eerie melody to accompany Jimmy's foul deed. He took a moment to breathe in the ocean air and ponder his next steps.

The first time he'd seen Hope Johnson, he'd known for certain their futures would be intertwined. He wasn't sure exactly how he knew, just that his former wife, in his former life, would often have visions of things to come, and after she passed on, it was as if he was waiting for some sign that she'd been right. He'd been alone for so long.

Instead of turning toward the Weller House, Jimmy returned to the saloon and took up playing piano until closing time. He heard whispers from some of the workers, including Charlie's assistant Clarence, and he put his power of influence to work. As he played piano, he began to send out tendrils from his mind, placing into the thoughts of the guests and those working that Charlie had been seen out back with one of the other bar owners in town and there'd been a scuffle. No one knew for sure which one drew their pistols first, but one of the men ended up dead and the other fled to avoid trouble with the police. Before the bar closed that evening, every one of the guests was chattering excitedly about old Charlie finally shooting someone with that pistol he'd won off of Beckett Smith in a card game back in the day. Jimmy had even taken the step to manipulate the chemistry of the beverages being served until each and every human soul in the saloon that night had experienced an evening of euphoria and tall tales before heading home to make love to their wives, husbands, mistresses, or assorted lovers. Jimmy made sure to cover his tracks so no one would suspect Hope, Bonnie, nor himself. He would deal with the women when he returned to the Weller House.

What he found when he entered his apartments at the back of the house stirred something inside him long dormant.

Hope and Bonnie lay sleeping soundly in his bed. They were facing each other with their foreheads pressed together and wrapped in a lovers' embrace. Jimmy sighed as he watched them sleep from his perch in an armchair by the window. Such beautiful women, and so much heartache they'd both experienced. He'd heard pieces of their tales as gossip between the workers at the saloon and had watched the two of them together when they thought no one was looking. People rarely noticed Jimmy unless he quit playing piano. That was the beauty of never speaking to anyone at the saloon.

But the Weller House was his home. Here, he was free to be himself, no hiding his true self, and boy were the women going to be surprised when they learned the truth about him.

Bonnie's red curls fanned out over the white pillows on his bed. She rolled onto her back and lifted her arms above her head to stretch, her thin white chemise hugging her body gently. Her breasts lifted with her intake of breath and Jimmy appreciated the sight.

Hope rolled over onto her side away from Bonnie and her

hands held her belly protectively. Through the thin white material of her chemise, Jimmy saw the twins moving. He knew she was having twins, although he wasn't totally sure why. The babies' hands and feet poked out and slid along her abdomen. One tiny foot shot out and made the material move. He smiled, his heart warmed thinking about how perfect their tiny hands and feet would be.

Bonnie rolled back over and spooned up against Hope's back, her hands joining Hope's on her belly. When another foot kicked out, Bonnie sat up with a start, her sleepy smile making her all the more attractive to Jimmy.

"They're so active this morning," Hope said sleepily. She yawned wide and rolled onto her back, smiling at Bonnie. Bonnie caressed Hope's belly and then leaned down to kiss her.

Jimmy couldn't help it, he squirmed in the chair as he fought the arousal he felt watching the lovers on his bed. It had been ages since he'd felt the rush.

Hope started at the sound of the chair squeaking and pulled frantically at the sheets to cover herself. Bonnie just raised an unappreciative eyebrow at him.

"You think it's appropriate to be watching us sleep, do you? What, are you some kind of creeper?"

Jimmy smiled and cleared his throat. "No, ma'am. But seeing as this is my room, where else do you suppose I should be this fine morning?"

Bonnie frowned. "Anyplace else."

"I'm afraid I can't do that," Jimmy said as he stood from the chair. He approached the bed and sat down on the edge nearest to Hope, who scooted away from him.

"Why did you bring us here?" Hope asked in a small voice. "Why did you save me?"

"Because you are meant to be here," Jimmy said, wishing he could reach for her bare foot sticking out from under the blanket and caress the arch with his thumb. "You wouldn't believe me if I told you, but you are meant to be here."

Hope blinked. She pushed herself to sitting a sitting position and winced.

"How are you feeling?" Jimmy asked her, wishing he could move closer. Bonnie got that protective look about her again and threw out a hand to stop him.

"I don't know what you want, Manwaring, but you better not touch her!"

There was a moment of tension that nearly broke Jimmy's resolve. He knew there was a reason Hope was here, and now that he'd realized that Bonnie was a part of the picture, he was unsure how to proceed.

Something changed in Hope's posture, and that tension seemed to dissipate.

"It's alright," she said to Bonnie and patted her hand. "He saved me from Charlie. In fact, I think he's been looking out for me, haven't you Jimmy?"

Jimmy nodded, waiting for her to go on.

"You knew, didn't you? That night I spoke to you."

"I did. I...felt them."

"What do you mean *felt*?" Bonnie asked. "Did you touch her?"

"No," Hope said calmly. "But you knew? And you know—"

"Twins. Yes. I sometimes just know things."

"Are you some kind of witch?" Bonnie asked.

A dark veil descended over Jimmy's face and both women recoiled.

"Are *you* that small-minded? You think anyone that is different is a witch?"

Bonnie swallowed. "I'm sorry, I just want Hope to be safe. Thank you. For rescuing her," she said, moving forward hesitantly to take Jimmy's hand. He reached for her, willing the darkness to recede. They shook hands and a jolt went through Jimmy, shaking him to his core. He hadn't felt that way since...

Bonnie sucked in a breath, but her grip tightened instead of letting go. They sat motionless, still holding hands and it was as if they wordlessly agreed they would work together to ensure Hope's and the babies' well-being. But Jimmy felt something more, that there was more to this situation than his dead wife had foreseen.

Jimmy let go of Bonnie's hand and stood from the bed. "You will both stay with me. I will ensure your safety and that of the children."

"But," Hope protested. "What about Charlie? Won't they be looking for me?"

"I've taken care of everything. Witnesses saw Charlie and another man fighting in the alley and saw Charlie pull his pistol and fire. As far as everyone is concerned, Charlie ran away to avoid the law and Clarence is the new owner of the Golden West Saloon."

The women gasped and looked at each other, confused.

"But how? How is it possible?"

Jimmy turned and walked for the door with a heavy heart. He knew the women would be safe, but he also knew he'd have to let them into his world, his existence, and he wondered if they would respond with revulsion, or worse...

"You'll understand soon enough," he said just before shutting the door.

5

---

ope and Bonnie sat on the bed silently for several minutes after the mysterious Jimmy Manwaring left the room. He'd always been peculiar, but now that he spoke, he was even more intriguing. It seemed as though he'd been expecting them, but that was just crazy, wasn't it?

Bonnie took Hope's hands in hers. "I know this is sooner than we planned, but we have some money saved up. We can leave this place and start over somewhere else. Maybe leave California even. We can go anywhere."

"We can't go just anywhere," Hope said. She wrapped her arms protectively around her squirming babies, who seemed to have settled since Jimmy left the room. "Tell me, Bonnie. Do you really want to leave here?"

Bonnie raised her eyebrows as if to protest. She opened her mouth to speak, but then she closed it. She looked around the room and Hope followed her gaze.

The bed was large, perhaps even king-sized, and it was made with delicate linens that had felt heavenly against her skin. The furniture looked very expensive and the window dressings were ornate. What was a piano player in a saloon doing living in a fancy place like this?

"It's not...I don't...I'm just worried for you, Hope. What do you think he wants from us? I don't want to end up with some man telling me what to do. I ran away to keep that from happening, and then I found you and look at what you've been through! I won't never let us be mistreated by a man again."

Hope was grateful for Bonnie for many reasons. She'd been the best friend she could have ever hoped for. She was protective and loving and always seemed to know what was best in every situation. But something about Jimmy had her feeling like they were exactly where they belonged. All of them. If she still prayed, she would have asked God what to do, but God left her to the mercy of an abusive man who nearly killed her and her unborn children. God hadn't been the one to get her to safety and provide a new life. That had been Bonnie. God hadn't saved her from the wrath of Charlie in the alley. Jimmy had done that. And what would happen with her babies remained to be seen.

Truthfully the idea of being in a safe place thrilled her. What if this man could truly take care of her and her children? She'd had to work so hard, had been through so many trials and tribulations in her life...didn't she deserve some peace? Didn't her children?

"Let's just hear him out," Hope said. "If he's not what he says he is, if he makes you feel uncomfortable at all, we're gone. Okay?"

Bonnie's shoulders slumped, only Hope couldn't tell if it was in relief or in disappointment.

A knock at the door startled them both.

"Hello? Ladies, I am Phoebe. Mr. Manwaring sent me to bring you fresh clothes. I am also to draw you a bath."

The short, slight woman breezed into the room with clothing draped over her arms and laid the dresses out on the end of the bed. They were lovely, simply made, and Hope touched them, soft as butter beneath her fingers. She and Bonnie smiled excitedly at each other.

"Phoebe? Can I ask you a question?" Bonnie asked.

Phoebe smiled. "You may ask me anything. I'll answer what I can."

The women looked at each other, and Hope could tell what Bonnie was thinking from one glance.

"Is Manwaring...is he on the up and up? He ain't some criminal or some bad guy, is he? Can we trust him? You know, woman to woman."

Phoebe took in a deep breath. "I've known Mr. Manwaring for many years. He brought me to work here for the Wellers several years ago. Mr. Manwaring keeps apartments here on the grounds, but the Wellers run the inn for guests of all walks of life. He's been nothing but generous to everyone here."

Hope breathed a sigh of relief. She wanted to trust her instincts that Jimmy was a good man, but hearing this woman speak of him put her at ease.

"Thank you, Phoebe," Hope said, offering the woman a smile. "I think I would very much like a bath."

"Very well," she said, turning for the bathroom. "If you will follow me through here."

Phoebe led Hope and Bonnie into a room attached to Jimmy's bedroom. In the center of the room was a large porcelain clawfoot tub. There was a toilet in the corner and even a wash basin with taps for running water.

"Mr. Manwaring had water piped into the house last year and had these fixtures installed recently. I'll run a bath for you now, then you may use the facilities as you need. I brought fresh towels up yesterday and any lotions or soaps you may need can be found in the cabinet above the sink."

Hope and Bonnie could not stop staring at the brilliant white gleam of the tub and toilet. Their dormitory had a water pump out back, and they used an outhouse behind the building. It wasn't pleasant, but as they didn't have to share it with the men, they'd been able to keep it quite clean. But this...this wonderful room was more beautiful than anything Hope had ever seen. She'd heard from guests passing through of such finery, but never imagined she'd be invited to use such a room herself.

"If there's anything you need, there's a bell on the dressing table in the bedroom. Ring it, and I will come. Mr. Manwaring will see you downstairs for breakfast when you are ready."

Phoebe turned and left the women to gawk at their good fortune.

"Is this for real, Bonnie?"

"Is *he* for real, is what I'm thinking. There's gotta be a catch. He wants something from us. I don't know if I can do this, Hope."

"What? What do you think—you mean sex? You think that's why he brought us here? Look at me! He would never look at me like that."

"Well, after you have the babies of course—"

"No, Bonnie, look at me. *You*, I understand. You are beautiful and your skin is perfect, your hair is lovely…"

"Oh, Hope. I wish you could see you how I do."

Bonnie approached her and placed her hands gently on Hope's shoulders. She slid the chemise from her shoulders and let it fall to the floor. Bonnie traced her fingers delicately over Hope's shoulders and down over her swollen breasts.

Hope shivered and then sighed happily at Bonnie's light touch. She felt so much love for her friend, and moments like these when they were alone and could be free to love each other were the best she'd experienced in her whole life.

After they bathed they dressed in the gowns Phoebe had brought for them. They were quite stylish, and Hope wasn't quite sure how the undergarments worked. The thin material didn't hide Hope's baby bump at all. They laughed together as they watched the babies roll around in Hope's belly.

"They are going to be so darn cute, Hope. I just know it."

Hope tried to imagine what her life would be like with her babies. It was a frightening future she faced, but with Bonnie she felt like she could handle it.

As for Jimmy, well, she'd just have to see about that.

6

Hope and Bonnie left the room and followed Phoebe's instructions to get to the dining room at the bottom of the stairs. Bonnie pushed open the door and there sat Jimmy drinking coffee in a starched white shirt with charcoal grey trousers on. His dark auburn hair was slicked back on his head and his pencil-thin mustache looked as if he'd shaved and trimmed recently, perhaps even this morning. He stood as they entered and gestured with his hand that they should join him, then moved around to pull out their chairs and push them into the table, taking care with Hope's swollen belly. As he sat back down, his dark gaze traveled between the two women.

"I don't know if I said thank you," Hope said to him in a voice just above a whisper. "I thought for sure—"

"He would have killed you if given a chance," Jimmy said to finish her thought. He took a long drink from his coffee and set his mug down. "I couldn't let that happen, but then I knew that rescuing you might put you in a heap of trouble as well."

Bonnie and Hope looked at each other with wide eyes.

"While we're grateful you saved Hope and the babes, and we appreciate your hospitality, we should probably..."

"And where will you go?" Jimmy asked. He let his hands drop in his lap and he watched her shrewdly, perhaps evaluating her intelligence.

"We've been saving money. We thought we'd travel to a different town, you know, start over."

He nodded at that and his gaze fell on Hope. Her skin heated in a way that seemed different from her temperature fluctuations brought on by the pregnancy. It was as if each sweep of his eyes over her chest and shoulders, which were exposed in this dress, warmed her like a breeze. Or like a caress, but like none she'd ever known. She inhaled and could smell a distinctly male scent, like some sort of woodsy aftershave lotion. The scent loosened her muscles and soon she found herself sliding down in the chair a bit, feeling as relaxed as she likely ever had. She couldn't help but sigh and smile at him, somehow knowing he was responsible.

Jimmy's lip twitched as though he too wished to smile, but then his eyes darted to Bonnie and her expression of consternation had him growing more serious.

"You're free to try a fresh start, but why not accept what I'm offering?"

Bonnie frowned at him. "What exactly *are* you offering? And what do you want in return?"

Jimmy reached slowly for his coffee mug and took a long couple of drinks. He set the mug down carefully and rested his hands on the table before him. Hope couldn't help but be mesmerized by how perfect his hands were. Plenty large enough to be considered masculine, able to perform manual tasks, but well cared for like a lady's. No dirt under his fingernails, nor mangled, scarred flesh like most of the loggers she'd seen in the bar. The backs of his hands were lightly covered by hair darker than that on his head. Hope wondered what his skin would feel like. She had never appreciated the touch of her husband because he always hurt her with his hands, always, but something about Jimmy set her at ease, almost from the inside out, so much so she felt herself close to dozing off in the warm sunlight coming through the window.

"I want to provide a home for you, make sure your needs are met, and I want to be present when the babes are born."

His words acted as cold water thrown on a sleeping form. Hope sat up straighter and narrowed her eyes at him.

"What do you want with my babies?"

Jimmy held up a hand. "I want nothing, only to be present to witness the miracle of life entering this world. My wife was unable to conceive a child..." His words drifted off and he cleared his throat. Hope watched as the darkness in his eyes took on a color almost, like a greenish hue, but that wasn't possible. His Adam's apple bobbed in his throat as he swallowed back what seemed to be a sob.

"What happened to your wife?" Hope asked softly, knowing it must be a terrible tale from his reaction.

Jimmy took in a deep breath and he got as close to a smile as she'd ever seen on him.

"Another time. You ladies enjoy your breakfast. We can talk more later." Jimmy stood to leave and Bonnie stood to face off with him.

"Just a minute. Now, we ain't agreeing to nothing until you tell us what you want, and don't tell me you just want to see her birth the babies! I don't want you thinking we belong to you or nothing. And don't you think for a second—"

Jimmy took a step toward her, but somehow his movement wasn't threatening. It was as if he were entering the space of a wounded animal and he knew just how to tame it. He stood close enough to Bonnie that she looked as though she wanted to step back, but instead she swayed toward him, brushing against him. She gasped and brought a hand to her chest. Jimmy shook his head and looked away.

"There are men who would take from you your choices. It is a woman's right to decide for herself. I have always lived by that creed, and I always will. I came from a place and a time where that wasn't true, and I'll be damned if I ever let that happen again."

Jimmy pushed past Bonnie and left the dining room. Hope heard him speaking to someone, possibly Phoebe, in the hallway and then the front door opening and closing. Hard.

Bonnie stood in her spot, unmoving, with a quiver in her jaw.

"What is it?" Hope asked, pushing herself to a standing position. She approached Bonnie and touched her arm, which seemed to wake her from some sort of trance.

"That man has seen unspeakable things," Bonnie said to Hope in a hushed voice.

"How do you know?" Hope asked her. She recalled several instances in the past where Bonnie had a strong reaction to someone and told Hope something similar. Hope wondered if she had a touch of the Sight, like Hope's grandmother did. That uncanny ability to sense things others didn't, and to see things sometimes better left unseen, was a gift and a curse to Hope's gran, and it seemed to be the same for Bonnie.

"When he touched me just now," she whispered. She grasped Hope's arm and Hope felt her trembling.

"What did you see?"

Bonnie's eyes grew wider and she shook her head as if to indicate she couldn't bring herself to share.

Hope felt a twinge in her back as the twins shifted inside her and she winced.

"I think I should lay down for a while. That fall left me a might sore."

"I'll help you upstairs. Perhaps that Phoebe will have some liniment to ease your pains."

Phoebe entered then with a tray covered with breakfast foods.

"Oh, I was just coming to bring you some breakfast. Are you feeling alright, miss?"

"Her back is bothering her. Is there any way you could bring that upstairs so I can feed her in bed?"

Phoebe smiled. "Of course. Mr. Manwaring asked that I show you around and bid you to make yourselves comfortable. His apartments are quite roomy, but you are welcome to use the house as you like. He means for The Weller House to be your home now."

Hope patted Bonnie's hand. "Actually, may we sit? And perhaps, Miss Phoebe, you can tell us about this place. We've only been in town a couple of months and we've not yet been to this part of town."

Hope just wanted to keep the woman talking and talk she did as she set down her tray, handed each of the women a plate of food, and then proceeded to tell the tale of how Mr. Manwaring had designed the house himself and built it a decade ago. Once it was completed, he hired the Wellers to run the inn, using their name and local celebrity to bring in the guests. Mr. Manwaring apparently enjoyed being around people, especially newlyweds, but preferred not to interact unless necessary. It was the first private home built on the bluff here, though others had sprung up in the past year or two, mostly to house the bosses over at the Union Lumber mill and their high society wives. The Wellers were wonderful businesspeople who cared for the wealthy who chose to visit their quaint logging town.

After they ate, Phoebe showed them the library just outside the dining room. A fireplace kept the room cozy and dry during these cool months. The shelves displayed many first editions of classic literature, sheet music collections, and several different versions of the Bible, the Book of Mormon, and the Doctrine and Covenants, which Hope found interesting. She'd had a Latter-Day Saint teacher in Independence, Missouri, and had studied the books as she learned to read. A day lost in books in the library would be such a treat.

The remainder of the bottom floor at the front of the house held three large guest rooms, all with separate bathrooms. Upstairs there were four more guest rooms and then a small washroom. On the other side of the washroom was a door that led to Jimmy's apartments. He had a sitting room, two bedrooms, and a bathroom to himself.

Another set of stairs led to a large ballroom on the third floor. Phoebe explained that it was used as a social hall for several Bible study groups, and when it wasn't used, Mr. Manwaring played the piano in the corner. Hope smiled as she ran her fingers along the wooden cover that hid the keys. She so loved the music he played. Perhaps he'd play for them sometime.

"I'm to see to the guest rooms now. Is there anything else you ladies will be needing?"

"Thank you, no," Hope said, smiling at the older woman. Phoebe looked to be in her late thirties or early forties with just the beginnings of grey hair and crow's feet at her temples.

Phoebe nodded, looked between the women curiously, and said, "You're both welcome to make yourselves at home throughout the house. Dinner will be served for you in the sitting room of Mr. Manwaring's apartment at six o'clock. He, ah, won't be going to the saloon tonight, so..."

The saloon. Hope hadn't thought about that awful place at all since she'd awakened in the downy softness of Jimmy's bed. If he wasn't going back, perhaps that meant he wasn't convinced the coast was clear.

7

Jimmy climbed the back stairwell to his apartments and opened the door to his sitting room at precisely six o'clock according to his clock that chimed at the very moment. His two charges sat nervously at the small table with dinner sitting on plates before them. Phoebe had followed his instructions perfectly.

"Thank you for waiting," he said, knowing perfectly well that he was right on time.

"Your mistress has been quite kind to us today," Bonnie said with a bit of a smirk. Jimmy knew she'd probably spent the entire day trying to make sense of his actions. He'd noticed she was a bit of a busybody while working at the saloon, but she was harmless.

"Not my mistress, but I'm glad." He couldn't help but be coy with her. He rather enjoyed the back and forth. She challenged him and wasn't ready to back down. She'd need that fortitude in the coming months, Jimmy figured.

He looked to Hope and detected an anxiousness about her that was more excited than fearful.

"And how are you feeling after a day of rest?" he asked Hope.

She grinned. "It's really beautiful here. Feels like a dream."

Bonnie made an impatient sound that caught Hope's attention. Jimmy could tell that Hope didn't want to upset her friend and was therefore being cautious.

Jimmy gestured to them to begin eating their food and the three ate in silence for several long minutes. Bonnie's and Hope's eyes darted back and forth between them. Jimmy's lip only twitched as he ate his meal, comforted by the company of these two strong women who he'd managed to unsettle with his behavior.

Suddenly the table jerked and Hope gasped. Jimmy and Bonnie sat wide-eyed staring at her.

"I'm so sorry. It was—"

"The babies," Bonnie said, laughing. "They always get more active when you eat."

Hope looked to Jimmy in apology and he just smiled. He was tickled by their presence. He sensed their happiness through whatever bond they shared and it warmed him like nothing since...

"What happened to your wife, Mr. Manwaring?" Bonnie asked. Jimmy tore his gaze from Hope and sighed.

"My wife died. Here, well, in the house that was here before. I've owned this property since..."

Jimmy closed his mouth. What was he doing? Was he really going to tell them his truth?"

"Listen, Mr. Manwaring—"

"My brothers and I were silver prospectors in Nevada Territory for several years before I met and married Julianna. We traveled for some time before settling here on the Northern California coast. Life was good for twenty years, until my wife made the mistake of sharing one of her visions with a guest she'd had over for tea. This guest happened to be the wife of one of the mill owners and in a position of power in the town. Soon it got around that the Banes living near the bluffs were witches, and that they had brought evil upon their town in the form of a blight affecting an area of the forest the mills had been heavily logging. When Julianna took ill, no one would help, and she passed." Yes, and despite his powers, he'd been unable to save her. "That was nearly forty years ago."

The women stared at him, dumbfounded. He knew the questions they must have.

"How much you have suffered," Hope whispered. "You must have loved her so."

Jimmy reached behind him to grab a tumbler and his carafe of scotch. He poured two fingers and drank it down, wishing the burn could soothe his weary soul still tormented by the last days of Julianna's life. Her fever had been so high she'd become nearly delirious, talking about her life in Reno before Jonah and his brothers had come. She cried for her mother and sisters, even her father. He poured another glass and was about to set the carafe down when Bonnie clinked her glass against his. He looked up into her serious face and she nodded for him to pour. Which he did.

Bonnie drank the scotch down with just a slight clearing of her throat to show her discomfort.

"Forgetting the fact you're claiming to be eighty-something years old, what's this about witches?"

Jimmy finished his dinner, debating how much more he should actually say. He wiped his face with the napkin and set it on the table next to him. Leaning back in his chair, he glanced to Hope to be sure she wasn't frightened, and found her eagerly listening, one hand resting on her swollen belly still moving under her dress.

"Witches is what narrow-minded people think any time someone is a little different. Julianna sometimes had visions about people. She could tell something about them just by touching their hand or even clothing they'd worn. I'm not positive, but I think it started around the time I met her." And here he was opening the door to more confessions. "The circumstances under which we met were...She saw some things."

"My gran had the Sight. She knew things." Hope looked at Bonnie and smiled as Bonnie took her hand. "Just like Bonnie sometimes has a feeling. Your Julianna must have been like that."

Jimmy laced his fingers together and placed them on his chest. "She wasn't a witch. And God bless her but she dealt with all of the ugliness I brought into her life, and she never hated me for any of it.

She didn't deserve what happened to her." His head hung forward and he closed his eyes tightly, fighting back the emotion always barely held at bay. Unable to keep his control, he stood quickly from the table, startling the women, and stormed out of his apartments and up the stairs to the third floor.

His piano. His refuge. He couldn't leave the women tonight. He'd heard too many rumors in town during his daytime errands. It was likely he'd have to steal them away in the dead of night to avoid any unwelcome visitors, but for now he just needed to play.

He sat down on the bench before his beloved keys and stretched out his hands and arms. The bench creaked beneath his weight. He'd been a beanpole of a young man when he and his brothers descended into the mine back in 1860, but the year spent below ground did strange things to his body chemistry and when he emerged, he was forever changed. He'd gained several inches in breadth, even a couple in height, but his size couldn't fully explain his strength. And while his body became powerful, his brain was altered to an unheard-of capacity. He'd been able to do tremendous things with his mind: influence others around him, keep an almost photographic record of his experiences, even manipulate the chemical makeup of things with just his thoughts. It hadn't been enough, though, in the end. Not to give Julianna the child she desperately wanted, nor to save her life.

He poured his heart out into the pieces he played, and soon his shirt was drenched with sweat and his hair fell into his eyes. He played so hard he didn't even notice the presence of his female guests until he stopped to reach for his scotch in the cupboard next to his piano. Bonnie was there to hand him a glass.

Hope sat next to him on the piano bench and her belly brushed his side. He felt a tiny kick from one of the babes, and it brought him a twinge of joy and one of sadness.

"May I?" he asked before placing a hand on Hope's belly. He knew it was incredibly forward to ask. Men didn't touch women who weren't their wives or kin, but then the link between himself and the women solidified as the hours passed. They just didn't know it yet.

Hope nodded and took his hand. She placed it on the underside below her belly button and immediately the twins' hands or feet rushed to meet his touch. Hope gasped and gazed up into his eyes questioningly.

"Why? Why do they react like this?"

Jimmy slowly slid his hand up and the twins' hands followed. A tear escaped each of his eyes, followed the contour of his cheekbones and down to his chin.

Bonnie moved to stand protectively beside Hope as if she still didn't trust that Jimmy wouldn't hurt her. She placed her hands on Hope's shoulders and began to massage gently. Hope relaxed against Bonnie and her eyes fluttered shut.

"You should rest," Jimmy said. He stood from the bench and bent to scoop Hope up into his arms. She started to protest, but he used a little of his influence to ease her into sleep. He carried her back down the narrow stairwell and into his apartment, placing her gently on the center of the bed. She rolled onto her side and fell fast asleep.

Bonnie tugged on his shirt and gestured for him to follow her into the living area. Once there, she chewed on a fingernail and began to pace.

"You know, I appreciate what you done for her and that you brought us here, but we really can't stay. I can take care of her, I can. And I will. I just need to get her out of town. I need to keep her safe. And the babies."

Jimmy stepped closer to her and placed a hand gently on her forearm, pulling her hand from her mouth.

"Let me take care of the both of you. You don't have to take on the world by yourself."

"I ain't about to count on no man to take care of us, that's for sure."

"Is it just me you hate, or is it all men?" Jimmy asked, crossing his arms over his chest. He stood at the ready to handle any verbal or physical attacks from her, and for some reason that seemed to aggravate her even more.

"Listen, you can try to sweet talk me like you done Hope, but I ain't her. I ain't never met no man who done anything for a woman 'cept give her grief. You ain't done much to change my mind about that."

Jimmy's lip twitched. "I did save her life," he said, purposefully sounding arrogant about it. He didn't know why, but he liked aggravating her. Perhaps it was that fiery red hair of hers, or the way her cheeks grew rosy when she got her ire up.

"You keep bringing that up," she said, poking him in the chest. "You ruin any good feeling I might have toward you with your cocksure attitude."

Jimmy held up his hands. "I don't want anything from you, either of you, except for you to accept my hospitality. How do you think you two will fare trying to make your way without a man? Things have changed somewhat from when I was young, and of course you have the vote and all, but when it comes to navigating all the ins and outs of life, it sure makes it easier when you have a man on your side. Sad, but true."

Bonnie growled and gave him a nasty look. She stormed over to the window and stared out into the blackness. The wind powered over the bluffs, rattling the windows, but the large house remained warm due to the heat from the stoves. Despite that, Bonnie seemed to catch a chill. Jimmy stood behind her but didn't touch her. He knew she'd sense if he used his powers of influence to warm or ease her, so he merely used his large presence and attempted to be non-threatening.

After several moments Bonnie spoke. "What happened today in town? You seemed off when you came back."

Jimmy exhaled. "There's talk. Folks wondering what happened. Clarence down at the bar seemed to think it strange that a couple of women went missing from the dormitories in the wake of Charlie's disappearance. It may be beyond my powers of persuasion to solve this situation. I think...I know, we should leave."

"We? And why—"

"I've told you why. You need me to secure safe passage for you. And I need to protect those children."

"But—"

"My wife."

Jimmy walked away from Bonnie and attempted to calm the darkness inside him at the thought of what happened to his beautiful Julianna, and what she saw. He sat on the chaise and put his face in hands, but no matter how many times he scrubbed at his face, he was unable to remove the sight of his dying bride from his mind.

He felt Bonnie's hand on his leg and heard her inhale sharply. He turned to look at her and watched as her body trembled and her breath came in jerky gasps. Even her eyes moved rapidly behind her eyelids.

"Bonnie?" Jimmy grabbed for her wrists and tried to wake her from whatever was happening. "Bonnie!"

Her eyes opened and for a moment, he felt his beloved returned to him. Then it was gone, but Bonnie stared at him wide-eyed as if she knew.

"You burned her."

Jimmy flinched and tried to pull away but she stopped him. "No. You did right by her, Jonah. You done her no harm. She wants you to protect them babies."

After Julianna passed, after those long hours of her thrashing about in pain and crying out for relief...after she made him promise that when *hope* came his way, he must promise to protect them...after she breathed her last rattling breath, he'd gone into a rage. He set fire to their house which sat on this very site. He couldn't bear to put her into the ground, but the scorched earth remained under the foundation he'd rebuilt with his own hands. He felt her presence in the timber he'd used to build the frame. He felt her love in the air around him. Until now it had kept him anxious and restless, grieving. But watching Hope sleep so soundly on his bed gave him a peace he hadn't felt since the early days with Julianna. He'd give anything to have that peace reside with him for longer than a few days. He'd lived such a long time already.

Bonnie came out of her daze and shook her head as if to clear it, but when she gazed back at Jimmy, he could tell she knew everything.

"I ain't never had a vision like that before," she admitted. "In the past it's always been just bits, fragments. But you..."

Jimmy waited for her to blow up, to try to wake Hope and make a run for it, but she sat still, staring at him through narrowed eyes.

"Well," she finally said. "I guess I'd a kept my mouth shut if I had secrets like yours."

"How much do you know?" he asked, he would have panicked if he didn't have such a strong feeling that all of this was as it was supposed to be.

Bonnie cocked her head to the side. "I know why you left Nevada. I know about the silver."

They stared each other down for a long time.

"Then you know what I agreed to do. You know I have to protect Hope and the twins."

"As do I," she answered him.

He turned to face her on the chaise. "Are you going to work with me or against me?"

Bonnie leaned against the back of the chaise and raised an eyebrow at him. "You going to try to get between her and me? I know men got needs."

Jimmy shook his head. "My needs are quite different from most men."

"How do you mean?"

Jimmy rested his elbow on the back of the chaise. "I need the energy more than the act."

"The energy? How so?"

"When two people, or more, are intimate, their act creates an energy force. That force feeds me, feeds that unnatural presence you detected when you touched me the first time. You've seen me, seen my past, so you know I never hurt anyone."

"Not like that, no. But you hurt folk."

Jimmy sighed. He had. He'd murdered Charlie. He'd killed to protect Julianna. He'd gone into that damned mine and unearthed such an unholy presence... He knew his brothers continued to hold the town, now called Reno, under their influence and he felt responsible for the wake of evil he'd left behind. William and Lionel were still there. He couldn't tell for sure what had happened to Nathaniel, and at times he still mourned the loss of the one brother he looked up to the most. The best thing he could do for Julianna was move her away from that awful place, even if it meant leaving her family. He'd just hoped he'd done enough to give her a happy life.

"If we're going to protect Hope and the twins, I need to know that you won't fight me, Bonnie. I won't get between you two and what you have. But I need to keep them safe. I made a promise."

Bonnie nodded. "And for that reason, I will agree." She stood and walked over to the bed. She undressed next to the bed to her chemise and climbed in beside Hope, wrapping herself around her lover.

Jimmy stretched out on the chaise and leaned his head back. He watched the women closely while he sent out tendrils of his influence to ensure they were safe. He altered the energy around the house to keep strangers away. The inn itself only hosted four guests this night and he sensed they were just retiring. He hoped they would partake of their usual evening activities. If he was going to be strong enough for the three of them and the twins, he was going to need all the power he could obtain from that sensual energy, and since he hadn't been with a woman himself in nearly a decade, he needed the energy of others to keep him, hence the nights at the saloon. There was enough fornication in that den of sin to keep his body humming with energy. The inn provided just enough to keep him settled. Without the saloon, he would have to find some other way.

8

——————

Bonnie watched Jimmy watching them until he finally closed his eyes. His long, powerful body barely fit on the chaise as he rested, though Bonnie knew that he didn't sleep soundly. She had to admit he was quite handsome, but she'd long ago realized that men did nothing for her 'cept to cause pain and anger. Everything she needed in life had come to her in the form of a woman. Trusting him went against everything she'd ever known, but she'd do it. After what she'd seen when she touched him, after everything he'd been through, she knew she'd finally met a decent man, an honorable man, despite the fact that he carried a darkness inside him that frightened and thrilled her at the same time.

She'd had visions since before she could remember, but nothing had ever given her such a rush than to feel what was buzzing under his skin. It called to her, tempted her, and she knew if she ever touched that force herself, she likely wouldn't be able to resist it's pull. How he'd fought against it all this time she had no idea.

Bonnie caressed Hope's belly and felt faint flutters from the babies, but nothing like whenever Jimmy, or Jonah, whatever his name was, was near Hope. Those little ones sure went bonkers when he was nearby, especially when he played that piano. It made Hope feel safe and happy, and that was what mattered. Bonnie was going to have to put aside her twinges of jealousy. This thing needed to work between the three of them, for the children's sake.

Hope stirred and turned to glance sleepily at Bonnie over her shoulder. "You done fighting with him?" she asked, a lazy smile on her lips. Bonnie couldn't help kissing her.

"For now," she whispered, taking the kiss deeper. Hope rolled over to face her, not breaking the kiss until her belly got in the way and she giggled.

"I think he's good," Hope said. "He's not going to hurt the babies."

"I know," Bonnie admitted. "He and I came to an understanding," she said, sliding her hands up the front of Hope's dress, which she hadn't removed before Jimmy had laid her upon the bed. Bonnie began unbuttoning the dress and slid the shoulders away, revealing Hope's slip. Her swollen breasts moved freely beneath the thin material, unlike the tight undergarments she'd been wearing to conceal her pregnancy at the saloon. Bonnie longed to be skin to skin with her. It had been so long, and even those few times they'd had the luxury of any sort of privacy, they'd had to stay mostly clothed.

Hope glanced toward the chaise and back at Bonnie as if to question her actions.

"Let me help you be comfortable," Bonnie whispered, kissing her softly. She sat up and helped Hope out of her dress, and then proceeded to remove hers, as well as her slip. She pulled the covers over them and slid Hope's slip up over her breasts giving her the access to massage them gently.

Hope murmured quietly and tangled her hands in Bonnie's hair. It had been too long since Bonnie had cut it and her curls were untamed, but she loved the feel of Hope's fingers gently dragging over her scalp and tugging on her hair.

Bonnie buried her face in Hope's ample bosom and lost herself to the feel of Hope's skin as she kissed and licked her lover. The first time she'd touched Hope, she'd been afraid she'd be rejected as had happened before when she'd misread a friendship with a woman, but

Hope had smiled and welcomed her loving touch. Over time she welcomed it more and more enthusiastically.

"I love you," Hope whispered to Bonnie just as Bonnie used her hand to bring Hope to orgasm. Bonnie held her as the waves traveled Hope's body, and she laughed breathily in her ear. "You better stop or we'll wake him," Hope whispered.

Bonnie pulled one of Hope's sensitive nipples between her teeth and nibbled. "I don't think he'd mind one bit," Bonnie said as she moved to the other breast. She'd seen glimpses of what Jimmy talked about when he said he needed the energy. In some small way, maybe he could gain some comfort as well. "This don't hurt you?"

Hope shook her head. "No, but everything is so sensitive. I feel like all you have to do is look at me sometimes and *that's* going to happen again. That slip the lady gave me to wear has been brushing against my skin all day and it felt real nice."

"Someday," Bonnie promised, "I'm going to buy you the nicest things to cover your lady parts. You'll feel that good all the time."

The women kissed and touched each other for hours until they were both sweaty from the exertion. For the first time they felt free to be together, even if Bonnie knew their safety in this place was only temporary. They didn't bother to dress. They allowed themselves to enjoy the feel of the cool air on their skin and fell asleep a tangle of arms and legs.

THE ROOM GREW LIGHTER despite the gray day outside. Bonnie woke before Hope and was startled to find Jimmy awake and watching them once more, only this time she didn't feel angry. She covered Hope's body in case she woke up and smiled slightly at Jimmy.

He nodded and stood quietly, leaving the room to give them privacy to get dressed.

When Hope woke, still smiling, they hurriedly dressed and met Jimmy in the dining room. His lip twitched when Bonnie made eye contact, but he didn't speak. He'd cleaned up somewhere because he was once again dressed like a gentleman, well-groomed and sophisticated.

They thanked Phoebe when she placed plates of eggs, fruit, and toast in front of them and she smiled. They ate in silence, but it wasn't uncomfortable. Somehow during the night they'd all accepted that this was to be their life now. The three of them, and soon, the twins.

A loud banging on the door caused Hope to spill her glass of orange juice and her eyes to bug out.

Jimmy stood with a frown and said, "Go upstairs. Lock the door to my bedroom."

He stormed out of the dining area as Hope and Bonnie looked to each other.

"We better do what he says," Bonnie said, sensing unrest outside the door to the kitchen.

The women carried their plates with them and left them on the counter before climbing the back stairs up to Jimmy's rooms. Bonnie locked the door and the two women sat on the chaise, holding hands for comfort. From this angle, they couldn't see the front of the house through the window so all they could do was wait for Jimmy to return.

His expression was grim when he unlocked the door shortly after.

"We need to leave tonight."

"But this is your home," Hope said. "Where will we go?"

Jimmy paced in front of them and stopped before the large picture window that overlooked the bluffs. "I have a friend that has a place where we'll be safe. I wired him yesterday that I might need to impose on him, and I expect he will answer today with no delay. He runs a hotel and saloon in Grass Valley."

"Who was outside, Jimmy?" Bonnie asked.

"The constable. He come looking for you two, said someone saw Charlie drag you out back before he disappeared. He just wanted to question you, but there's too much suspicion out there that one of you had something to do with it."

"But how did the constable know we were here?"

"He didn't," Jimmy said. "And I want to keep it that way. The Wellers will keep this place in my absence, and we'll go where the path leads us."

Jimmy rang a bell and Phoebe appeared in the doorway.

"Pack my things," he said quietly to her. "I'll need you to pick up just a few more items of clothing for Miss Johnson and Miss Collins. We'll leave tonight."

"Tonight?" Hope said, wringing her hands in her lap. Bonnie hated the fear in Hope's voice. She also didn't like the idea of her traveling.

Jimmy must have sensed her unease as well. "I know this is not the ideal situation. I'd like to keep you here and out of harm's way, but once again this town is proving to not be the safe haven I desire."

Bonnie thought about the fools who'd shunned his wife in her time of need and wished to comfort him. As that wasn't possible, she had to be content with harboring some anger on his behalf and focus her comfort on Hope. She needed it most right now.

THE PLANS WERE SET. Pierre—the man Jimmy hired to manage the inn—would drive them to Santa Rosa, where they would then take a train to Sacramento, switch lines to Nevada City, and Jimmy received word that his friend from Grass Valley would meet them and bring them to the hotel. It went off without a hitch, but it was a long journey.

They arrived two days later and Hope was exhausted. Jimmy carried her up the stairs to their suite while Jimmy's friend's assistant, Delbert, brought their belongings from the car.

Bonnie had been pleased with the level of extravagance Jimmy poured upon them as they traveled. He made frequent stops for them to eat, ensured their travel upon the train was in a private car, and promised that once they arrived in Grass Valley, he would buy them each a new wardrobe. Hope had tried to protest, but Bonnie understood and knew that Jimmy had amassed a wealth over the past eighty years that allowed him to take care of their needs.

Their suite had a room with a large bed and a sitting room off to the side with a chaise. Delbert brought their things and was out of the room shortly to give them their privacy with a large wad of bills from Jimmy. Once the door closed, the three of them looked at each other.

"I'll just leave you two to, um, take care of your—"

Bonnie was too tired for modesty. She took off her coat, unzipped her dress and let it fall to the floor. She knew Jimmy would respect their agreements made before they left Fort Bragg.

Hope stared at Bonnie and then at Jimmy and slid out of her coat. She kept sneaking glances over her shoulder as Bonnie undressed her.

"Let me run you a bath," Jimmy said, obviously needing something to do. Bonnie watched him go into the bathroom, looking them over as he passed. Not exactly leering, but not trying to hide his admiration for them.

The water came on and Hope yawned. Her bath would have to be quick and then to bed with her.

"How are you feeling, my love?" Bonnie asked her.

"Everything just sort of aches," she said, her eyelids fluttering. Bonnie worried she would fall over if she didn't get her into bed soon.

"The bath will feel wonderful," Bonnie assured her as she led her into the bathroom.

Jimmy had rolled up his sleeves and was testing the water. "I think this temperature should be good for you. Hope, can I help you in? It's sort of a high step."

Bonnie spoke for her. "I think that would be fine. I don't want to chance it if I'm not strong enough to catch her."

Jimmy stood with his hands on his hips, unsure of his next step. Hope looked to Bonnie and then to him before nodding to Bonnie. Bonnie lifted her slip over her head, leaving Hope naked before Jimmy. The look of admiration in his eyes nearly floored Bonnie. It was in that moment that she knew just how affected he was by Hope. He appreciated her beauty as a woman and a mother-to-be.

Hope turned and held a hand out so he could support her stepping into the tub. He used both hands; one under her arm and the other around her waist, to be sure she didn't fall. Bonnie picked up a washcloth and a new bar of soap and created a lather. Jimmy stepped back and let her kneel next to the tub.

"I'll just be outside if you need anything," Jimmy said, his gaze saying he wanted nothing more than to stay.

"Please," Hope said from the tub. "Stay. The twins are much more at ease when you are near." She slid down in the tub and rested her head on the ledge with her eyes closed.

Bonnie gave him a welcoming glance and continued washing Hope's weary body.

Jimmy knelt down beside her and watched Bonnie's hands carefully. She could sense his desire to be a part of comforting Hope and the twins so she elbowed him gently, urging him to do what he wanted.

Jimmy rolled up his sleeves further and watched for Hope's reaction as he reached below the water and grasped her foot. Hope giggled as Jimmy concentrated hard on massaging her foot. Bonnie finished washing and moved behind her to rub her shoulders and neck. Soon Hope was completely relaxed, but the twins were wide awake.

"Oh!"

Bonnie and Jimmy watched as a foot, clearly outlined under Hope's skin, traveled the width of her belly. Hope giggled and touched the foot as it made it across. Soon, what looked like an elbow made it across from the other direction. Jimmy reached out a finger and his touch caused a maelstrom of activity.

"Would you look at that," Bonnie said, wrapping her arms around Hope and nuzzling her cheek. "They are so interested in you, Jimmy."

Bonnie was amazed at the sheer joy on his face. He wasn't exactly smiling, but his eyes lit up and he leaned even closer.

"What does that feel like? Does it hurt?" he asked Hope.

"It feels funny. Not pain, just strange."

"It looks like a miracle," Bonnie said, kissing her once more.

"They are so strong," Jimmy murmured. He splayed his large

hand over her belly and the hands reached up seeming to try to grasp his fingers. Hope giggled, but it turned into a yawn.

"We need to get you out before you prune," Jimmy said. He stood and reached for a towel. Bonnie supported Hope as she got to her feet and the two of them helped her step from the tub. Jimmy handed the towel to Bonnie to dry her off and took his leave from the room.

The women stood in silence until the door shut and then Bonnie turned Hope to face her.

"I'm sorry, I should have asked you—"

"It's fine. He is...well he's so different. And he's so caring. And the babies just want him near. They're always more excited but also they calm when he is near, it's the strangest thing. It's like his presence makes them happy."

Bonnie bent and dried Hope's legs. "As long as he's not making you feel uncomfortable. I won't allow it. I won't—"

"Does it make you uncomfortable? Him being here? Because I know how you feel about men."

Bonnie shrugged and grabbed the dressing gown she'd brought into the bathroom with them. She lifted it over Hope's head. "I thought I would be, but you're right. He's different. And he promised he wouldn't try to come between us."

Bonnie turned Hope to face her and kissed her. She smoothed Hope's hair back and thought again how much she wanted to pamper her.

"I know we just met him, Bonnie, but he's really sort of wonderful."

Bonnie paused with her hands on Hope's shoulders. "He is wonderful. But Hope, there's a...darkness to him. I told you he's seen some terrible things. He really has. Just be careful with him. I believe we can trust him as far as it's possible to trust a man, but he's not merely a man. He's something else."

Hope stepped back and frowned at Bonnie. "What do you mean he's something else?"

Bonnie didn't know how to answer that without scaring the wits out of her friend, so she simply opened the door for her and led her to the bed.

Jimmy had stepped out the door onto their balcony and through the window Bonnie saw him staring off into the distance. She wondered what heavy thoughts he carried, what sorrows and burdens he bore on his broad shoulders. For some unknown reason, she wanted to know him, know his soul. He was a spirit not unlike her; he was world weary, downtrodden. It was as if the world had punished him for a long time for things out of his control. Bonnie could relate.

Bonnie tucked Hope into bed and realized just how much she, too, needed to bathe. She stripped and bathed quickly, wanting nothing more than to curl up behind Hope and sleep for years. She left the bathroom in just a towel and paused.

Jimmy was sprawled on the small sofa in the sitting area with an arm thrown over his eyes. He couldn't have been comfortable. They'd have to discuss their sleeping arrangements in the morning.

9

Hope woke up stiff and sore. The days of travel were a lot for her poor body to handle in her condition. She tried to stretch out but Bonnie was curled up so close she didn't have much room to move. She climbed from the other side of the bed to use the bathroom, grateful for the luxury Jimmy had provided for them. She pulled the sheer curtains around the large canopy bed behind her to provide Bonnie just a little more time to rest.

She hadn't had much opportunity to look around at the hotel as she'd been exhausted when they arrived the day before. Now she appreciated the colorful flowers on the wallpaper, the intricate tile on the floor, and the shiny porcelain of the tub. A set of delicate lace curtains covered the bathroom window and an ornate glass orb covered an electric light above the mirror. Hope pushed the curtains aside and looked out the window. Rain pelted the glass and the sky was filled with angry-looking gray clouds. It was the kind of day that she'd always loved as a child because it meant snow was coming soon, but also that she would be permitted to stay indoors and read her books.

Books. She'd left the saloon in such a rush, her possessions had been forgotten. There hadn't been much other than the few rags she wore to work in, a picture of her family, and the two books she'd read cover to cover many times: The Wonderful Wizard of Oz and The Secret Garden. She'd wanted to cry for her books when she realized their loss during the journey here, but she was so grateful to Bonnie and Jimmy for looking after her, she couldn't exactly cry over lost belongings. She knew for a fact that Bonnie had also left behind her mother's hair comb and a shawl her grandmother had made for her before she left for her wedding. The wedding that never took place.

Hope often wondered if Bonnie hated men so because she'd been forced to marry an old widower with several small children and a cruel reputation. If not that, had she been mistreated as a young girl? She'd never say, only remarking that she had no use for men 'cept carrying in the wood for the stove.

Hope did not hate men as a rule. Not after being beaten and abused by her husband, nor after Charlie laid his hands on her. She held no hatred in her heart for the opposite sex. She even remembered being sweet on a boy at church years ago. She loved her father and was devastated when he passed away. He'd never have let the horrible man she'd married treat her rough. But with Daddy gone, she'd had to take matters into her own hands. She'd sworn the next time her husband came after her with his evil intentions, she'd knock him upside the head with her rolling pin. That's exactly what she'd done, however, how could she have known the exact spot on a man's head that if hit with a blunt object would cause a fatal injury? All she could do was run with the little money they had or spend the rest of her life in jail. That wasn't an option. She knew by then she was pregnant.

And now she was running once more because of the death of another man. This time she'd had no part in his demise, but it didn't matter one bit. This one fell squarely on poor Jimmy's shoulders. He'd only been trying to help her, and now he was stuck with her and the babies.

Funny how he didn't seem upset about that at all. For some reason, Jimmy acted as though this was all meant to be, just like setting a lit match to paper will cause a fire. All you can do is stand back and watch it all burn.

Hope returned to the darkened room and felt hunger pangs in her belly. The babies were restless and she felt a dull ache in her lower back that seemed to throb in time to her heartbeat. All she wanted was more sleep, but she knew the hunger would keep her awake.

She hated to wake Jimmy, but she was at his mercy. She had no money, only two changes of clothes, and had no idea where they were. He'd told them Grass Valley had been a mining boom town and now was mostly a quiet place folks passed through on their way to leisurely pursuits in the Sierra Nevadas, or to Sacramento to conduct business. The hotel they were staying in, The Holbrooke, was a holdover from the mining days and had even possessed an exchange at one point. Jimmy explained that his old friend Joaquin Del Oro currently ran the hotel and assured him that his new family could stay as long as necessary.

That's all he would tell them, however. Hope was curious and a bit anxious about this change in circumstances, but it was the inability to care for herself and her unborn children that concerned her the most.

Hope padded silently over to the sitting area of the suite and her heart sank at poor Jimmy slumped on the couch, still in his traveling clothes. His hair hung down over one side of his face, his full lips parted slightly. She'd never seen a man with his coloring before. His dark auburn hair looked almost black with the pomade he used to slick it back, and the result made him look so dramatic. His long nose, dusted with tiny freckles, gave him an aristocratic look, but he was anything but pretentious. The home they'd just run from was beautiful, but not unwelcoming. Jimmy seemed, for all intents and purposes, to be a decent, caring man, if a little mysterious. And just as the twins were physically drawn to his presence, so was their mother.

Hope felt a little lightheaded from lack of food. She couldn't put it off any longer. She patted Jimmy's hand gently and waited to see if he'd stir. Nothing. The man slept like the dead. "Jimmy?" she whispered.

Jimmy sat up with a start and gasped. "What's wrong? Are you alright?"

His eyes were so wide, she couldn't help but chuckle. "I'm fine, but these babies are sure hungry. I'm sorry to wake you—"

"No, no don't apologize. I'll go downstairs and speak to Joaquin's manager. He'll send some food from the kitchen."

Jimmy stood and towered over Hope. For a moment he stood close enough to touch her, and then his lip twitched in what she took to be his version of a smile, and he stepped away to right his clothes. Hope watched him stroll into the bathroom and really appreciated the way he moved. He was incredibly graceful and every movement he made telegraphed his power.

When he emerged from the bathroom, he glanced at Bonnie sleeping soundly on the bed and then his eyes found Hope.

"Lock this door behind me, and do not open it, ever, unless it is me. We're going to have to be cautious here as well."

Hope nodded and crossed the room to lock the door as he instructed. There was a peephole in the door that allowed her to watch him walk down the stairs. He pulled out a pocket watch and checked the time before turning the corner.

Hope passed the time waiting for him to return by looking over the bookcase in the sitting area and was pleased to find some books she recognized, although most of them were historical records from the town. If it wouldn't have been raining, she would have loved to sit outside on the balcony and read to her heart's content. Instead she sat on the chaise where Jimmy slept and leaned back into the cushions. She could smell faintly his unique combination of scents and she smiled. He smelled so good, he looked so dashing...and here she was a pregnant woman, a pregnant *colored* woman who had no business having any thoughts toward him other than gratitude.

Jimmy returned soon after with the man who'd greeted them the previous day, Joaquin. Both men carried trays piled high with food.

The man greeted her with a kind smile at the door and waited while Jimmy set his tray down and then returned for the second one.

"Let me know if there is anything else I may do to make your stay enjoyable."

Hope thanked him and then felt Jimmy's presence behind her.

"It is good to see you, old friend," Jimmy said, shaking the man's hand.

"And you as well. I look forward to catching up. Perhaps this evening? My wife and I would like to host you and your lady friends for dinner in our private room downstairs."

Jimmy nodded. "We would love to join you. However, I would appreciate it if our presence here was kept quiet, especially the women. Miss Johnson need not be disturbed in her present condition."

Joaquin shook his head. "No, that would not do. My wife can be trusted to keep your confidence, old friend."

Jimmy thanked him once more and then closed the door, locking it.

Bonnie stirred in the bed but did not wake, and Hope appreciated having the few moments alone with Jimmy.

He sat with her at the small table in the sitting area and sipped slowly from a cup of coffee while Hope tried not to make a pig of herself eating the delicious sausage and eggs with biscuits and gravy. She nearly finished the entire plate before she paused. She glanced up to see Jimmy watching her with amusement.

"I apologize for my horrible manners, but I just can't seem to get enough to eat some days."

"I can imagine. How are you feeling otherwise?"

She grinned over her coffee cup. "Excited. Scared. I can't wait to be a mother, but I worry..."

Jimmy smiled. "You're going to be wonderful, and with Bonnie to help, those babies will be spoiled." His smile slipped and he cleared his throat. "Hope? I know I'm not, well, I know I'm not their father...I just want..."

Hope laid her hand over his. "I want that, too."

Somehow, she knew what he was trying to say, that he wanted to be a part of their family, not just her guardian. She didn't think she knew just how that would work, but she wanted him there. The more time she spent with him, the more she was attracted to his smiles, his serious gazes. The beautiful music he made with his fingers that called to her very soul.

"What I want," Jimmy began, "I don't know that I have the right."

Hope frowned. "What is it?"

Jimmy placed a hand over the top of her hand. "When the time is right, I will discuss it with you. I fear you and Bonnie do not trust me enough yet for me to ask this of you."

"Ask what?"

Bonnie had joined them, rubbing her eyes. She yawned so widely her jaw cracked. Jimmy stood and pulled out a chair for her, which she took with a smile. Hope didn't miss the way his hand grazed the back of Bonnie's shoulder and the shiver it caused her.

"How did you sleep?" Hope asked, hoping to change the subject.

Bonnie turned to look at her and yawned once more. "Fine. I slept just fine. But what is it you two were talking about?"

"The twins. I wanted to reassure Hope that she would be well cared for here. Joaquin's niece is a midwife, and I've asked him to have her round to see you in the next day or two. My wish is that we remain here until they are born and then we can move on."

"You mean here? In this fancy place?" Bonnie asked. "Can you really afford all that?"

"You let me worry about the cost. I told you, Joaquin Del Oro is a friend, one who owes me a debt of gratitude. He and his family will protect us as long as we need them to. They are...powerful...in these parts."

Hope wasn't sure exactly what he meant, but Bonnie nodded as though that was all she needed to hear.

10

Jimmy spent his evenings playing the piano downstairs. He and his charges had been at the Holbrooke for two weeks now, and he sensed the women growing restless up in the room. Joaquin offered to close the restaurant and put out the "no vacancy" sign so they could come downstairs and move about, but Jimmy still feared for their safety. He'd felt the presence of something dark lurking near the inn, and he didn't want to bring any darkness into Hope's life presently. She was close to delivering the babies, according to Joaquin's niece Miranda, a skilled midwife. She said it could be within days.

Joaquin's family could be trusted to be discreet, so Jimmy allowed Miranda and her mother Carmen to visit with his women. *His* women. He'd certainly come to think of them that way. He'd sat by and listened as Miranda explained what they could expect during the birth of the twins, an event she'd witnessed many times. He desperately wanted to think he'd be present for more than just their births, but he'd yet to broach the subject with his women.

Joaquin's wife Dolores was a delightful woman and a storyteller extraordinaire. Jimmy loved seeing Hope and Bonnie paying such rapt attention to her tales of when she met Jimmy for the first time.

She and Joaquin had been in San Francisco on their honeymoon when they came across this fantastic piano player in the hotel lobby. They bought him drinks and after he finished playing, they spent hours talking until the sun came up. As they were all in the hotel business, they'd had that in common. What she didn't tell his women was that they had another more sinister connection.

Joaquin had been paid in silver coins from Reno, Nevada, by one of his guests.

Thinking them to be special, he'd kept them close to him, only showing his wife. They began noticing the differences soon after: Joaquin's arthritis disappeared, Dolores's lungs, damaged after a bout with pneumonia, bothered her no longer. They found themselves changing, growing stronger, their business booming. When they confessed all of this to Jimmy upon his first visit to their hotel, he'd become so angry. How had the coins gotten away from his brothers like this? Were they being so careless now to just give the silver to anyone? It had almost been enough of a motivation to go to Reno in person and let them have a piece of his mind, but he wasn't ready to face them yet. Not until he was stronger. Not until he was sure his women, and the precious babies, were safe.

He also learned during one of his visits with his new friends that the Del Oro family possessed their own bit of magic. Certain members in each generation had been born with gifts and they practiced a form of witchcraft called *brujería*. Joaquin's sister Carmen and her daughter Miranda were both very powerful, and they'd assisted Joaquin and Dolores in accepting the changes to their lives. Jimmy had found them to be charming and knowledgeable and had shared his family's dark secret with them. It had been a relief to have found allies in his many years of walking the Earth alone.

Hope had accepted Jimmy's wishes that they remain behind closed doors. She hadn't felt up to exploring anyway and spent most of her days resting in bed and dozing, her energy flagging from the demands of the babes. Bonnie had been more difficult to contain. Several nights while the rest of the hotel slept, Jimmy had awakened to find her stepping out of the door and onto the balcony out front to gaze at the moonlight. He hated to take the fresh air from her, so he'd pretend to sleep through it rather than confronting her. He saw no harm in her actions and knew he was close if anything went wrong. But his unease remained, lurking in the corners of his consciousness like the very darkness he feared.

The nocturnal activity of the hotel guests was not quite at the level he needed to absorb to remain at full strength and he felt the weakness at times. He hadn't slept well either, giving the bed to the women and opting to sleep with his limbs dangling from the too-small chaise. Hope insisted he needed a bed to rest in, but he'd fought her. She was the one who needed the rest.

The darkness he'd been sensing flickered at the back of his awareness this night, and he stood abruptly from the piano, startling the night manager at the desk. A few voices hollered from the saloon for him to keep playing, but he politely declined and turned for the stairs.

As he approached the door to their suite he heard raised voices. He nearly broke down the door when his hands couldn't work fast enough to unlock it. When he burst in, he found Bonnie pacing next to the bed and Hope clutching her belly.

"What's wrong? What's going on?"

Bonnie planted her fists on her hips. "She's having the pains and I told her we needed to call the midwife, but she won't listen."

Jimmy approached Hope and she held out a hand to him. He took it and sat on the bed next to her.

"It's not time. I don't know, I can just tell. The babes are restless. Will you stay?" she asked. "They are always more at ease when you are near."

Jimmy looked to Bonnie, who nodded, though she didn't seem happy about it.

"What can I do?"

Hope lay back on the pillows with a wince. "Lay beside me. Please, Jimmy. I know it's not time yet, but they need to be calmed."

Unsure, Jimmy moved a little closer, but he was hesitant. He'd been careful not to interfere with Hope and Bonnie's intimacy, and the bed was theirs. He was afraid to intrude.

As if she could read his mind, Bonnie slid out of her dress and climbed onto the bed on the other side of Hope and reached for Jimmy's hand, placing it on Hope's belly. She sucked in a breath and the babes moved around, causing her discomfort.

"Closer. Please," she whispered. "They want you, Jimmy."

Fascinated, Jimmy lay by her side, his body crying out in relief to finally be in a comfortable place and yearning to be close to the babies. He turned on his side and curved to her side, resting his hand on her belly. She sighed with relief.

"I wish you could play piano for them," she whispered as she gazed up at him with dark eyes full of wonder. "I love to hear you play."

Jimmy smiled. He glanced at Bonnie who had molded her body to Hope's other side.

"Sing for them, Jonah," Bonnie said, using his given name. She did that sometimes, letting him know she understood how he was feeling.

He closed his eyes, resting his head next to Hope's on the pillow and began to sing the first song to come to him. It was a hymn his mother had taught him as a young man. He kept his voice low but poured as much emotion into his words and melody as he possibly could. His energy flowed through his connection to Hope's body and he concentrated it into her womb.

Hope sucked in a breath and then smiled as she exhaled, sinking deeper into the pillows and falling asleep. She rolled onto her side facing Bonnie and the two kissed gently. Bonnie caught Jimmy's eye and reached for his hand once more, pulling his arm over Hope and resting it on Bonnie's hip.

The contact flooded Jimmy's body with such a sense of warmth, connection, and peace. He'd yearned for this for decades. Since the loss of Julianna, Jimmy hadn't felt this close to another, and his heart felt as though it might just burst from his chest.

He wanted to be close to Hope, and he cared for and respected

Bonnie. These women meant the world to him and he would do anything to keep them safe.

They dozed together, their bodies pressed against each other in an intimate manner. Jimmy dreamed of the three of them together like this with two dark-haired beauties crawling over them in bed, waking them on a sunny morning. Bonnie and Hope laughed while Jimmy pretended to be a snarling monster ready to eat small children who wake him from his slumber. He scooped them up and snarled against their necks while they squealed in laughter and struggled to get away. Bonnie rescued them as Hope kissed Jimmy good morning and sank into his embrace. Bonnie took the babes from the room giving Jimmy and Hope a moment alone to enjoy each other's bodies. In the dream, Jimmy made love to Hope tenderly and the smile on her face was so serene and loving…

Jimmy woke suddenly and felt a chill. The room was pitch black except for a faint greenish glow near the door to the balcony. Something in the pit of his stomach recognized that glow and was drawn to it despite knowing in his heart and mind it was evil.

Jimmy rose from the bed and walked toward the door, his sleepiness falling away with every step. He placed his hand on the doorknob and turned it, the cold seeping into his bones.

Outside the brisk air made him shudder. In a chair at the far end of the balcony, a dark figure sat, his feet kicked up on the railing. Smoke drifted up from a lit cigar. Jimmy moved closer, his bare feet numb from the icy balcony boards beneath his feet. It was mid-October, but already feeling like winter this night.

The green glow flared as Jimmy approached and the man chuckled. "I wondered if my presence was enough to draw you from the warmth of your women." He puffed once more on the cigar and tilted his head back to blow out the smoke, accompanied by green flames. He wore a large, brimmed hat low over his eyes casting dark shadows over his face so thick Jimmy couldn't make out any features save the greenish hue where eyes would be. The voice that emanated held no humanity. It was the sound of the evil the four brothers unearthed all those years ago. Jimmy would never forget that sound.

"What are you?" Jimmy asked, bracing himself against the unsettling feeling that ran down his arms and legs until he could no longer move.

"You don't need to ask that, young Jonah. You know what I am."

"I know you don't belong here."

"And *you* do?" The creature chuckled and the dread churned in Jimmy's stomach. "You have such nerve for one so vulnerable. Tell me, how's your strength been?"

Jimmy shuddered as he felt a wave of icy fire brush against his exposed skin.

"You don't need to ask. You already know."

That chuckle again. Jimmy fought the urge to vomit.

"I know that I have missed you. You have been gone for too long. You grow weak." The creature leaned close. "Your brothers miss you."

The place in his heart Jimmy kept closed off from his conscious thoughts flung wide open. The pain nearly crippled him.

"What do you want?"

"What I always want. You. All four of you. I've spent time intimately with your brothers, but I've missed you. I hoped you would return before now."

Jimmy fought against the pressure holding him in place and tried to stay calm enough to breathe. His lungs felt as though they would collapse under the pressure.

"My life was in Fort Bragg." That's all he was able to say.

"Your life belongs to *me*," the creature hissed. "And I want it. I want you back close to me."

Jimmy swallowed down the bile in his throat. "I can't. I'm needed."

"You are needed where *I* need you to be."

"I made a promise," Jimmy growled.

"A promise you shouldn't have made. And yet you did. So that is a problem. You have two women and two babies in the womb under your care, and yet you owe me."

"I owe you nothing! You took everything from me!" He turned his back on the darkness and meant to leave, meant to return to the warmth inside the room.

The creature pressed up against his back and Jimmy nearly screamed in pain from the burn.

"You belong to me, Jonah Call. Jonah Bane. Jimmy Manwaring. Whatever you choose to call yourself, you belong to me. And I *will* have you."

"I made a promise!"

Jimmy gasped in pain as the green flames surrounded him and long forgotten feelings rushed to the surface. The rush of power, both agonizing and exhilarating simultaneously, sucked all of the oxygen from his body and prohibited him from screaming.

"I would never make you break a promise, young Jonah. There's plenty of room in Reno for you and your new family. All you have to do is bring them once the children are born and it is safe for them travel. It's simple." The creatures grip tightened enough to make Jonah gasp once more.

"What do you want with them?" Jimmy croaked.

"The same thing *you* want from them. You just won't admit it."

Jimmy froze. Did he want something? Was he doing this for some other reason than the promise he'd made Julianna?

Yes. He cared for the women, both Hope and Bonnie. If he was honest with himself, he was incredibly attracted to them both, but in very different ways. Hope's energy had called to him the moment she stepped foot in the saloon. Just as her name implied, she was everything good and positive that Jimmy had missed since losing his Julianna. She was beautiful; her teasing smile and bright eyes gave her a welcoming aura, like a warm hug after a long walk in the cold. And while Jimmy hadn't spent much time around pregnant women, he was surprised at how aroused he became around her. As her belly grew and stretched, the swell of her hips and breasts made him nearly breathless when he watched her...really watched her. He loved watching her and Bonnie sleep together side by side, her babes protected between them.

And Bonnie...Her fire warmed the parts of him left out in the cold all these years. He loved verbally sparring with her and enjoyed the hours they'd spent talking and laughing. Her natural distrust of all things male gave him plenty of ammunition in their debates, and her thoughtful, if sometimes petulant, responses entertained him to no end. He knew she did not desire him physically, but if he were a betting man, he'd put his money on him being someone she'd come to trust and admire, if only platonically. And he'd take that if it meant she'd remain in his presence for as long as possible.

The bottom line was that Bonnie and Hope, along with the twins, were a package deal, and they were a package he'd sworn to keep safe, and had grown to love.

"What is your answer, young Jonah?"

What could he do? The creature had come this far and could find them again. What he was asking wasn't going to harm Jimmy's charges, now was it? Jimmy had already asked to be present when the babies were born, knowing that their entry into the world would be an act of love in its purest form, and he wanted to bask in it.

The creature, on the other hand, would feed on their innocence. He couldn't hurt them. Jimmy would never allow them to be touched, nor to touch the cursed silver that would ensnare them as it had done Jimmy and his brothers. The creature could feed from them, and it wouldn't hurt them, would it?

Years before, when Julianna was still alive, a young couple had come to stay at their small inn, and the mother gave birth somewhat prematurely. They thought they'd had more time, but the baby was determined. Julianna had acted as midwife since the town doctor couldn't arrive fast enough, and Jimmy, then Jonah Bane, had been just inside the room, ready to lend a hand. When the child took its first breath, Jimmy staggered under the rush of energy the tiny being emitted. The love in such a pure form that passed between first mother and child, and then father and child as he cut the umbilical cord, brought tears to Jimmy's eyes, and a flood of power to his being. It was different than the carnal energy he gained from being near when two or more people fornicated, and different than when he himself partook of the flesh, but still was enough to boost his strength and fill him with virility. The feeling was different, the outcome the same, and it had taken him a long time to not feel guilty or dirty for needing it, wanting it. He couldn't change who or what he was after all these years. Best to just make do and try not to leave a negative impact on anyone in his life.

"If you promise not to touch the children, or the women...If you swear that you will never attempt to seduce any of them with your wretched influence nor harm them in any way...I will come back to Reno."

The crushing sensation evaporated, and Jimmy sucked in as much air as his lungs could hold. His body was starved for oxygen. He knew he'd just made what was near enough to a deal with the devil, but he felt he'd had no choice in the matter. If he didn't cooperate, those he cared for...loved...would be hurt in the process. Best to go along with it and hope for the best. He just prayed with the bit of humanity he'd managed to hold onto that the creature would honor his end of the deal.

"Very well, young Jonah. If it means having you back once more with your brothers, I will accept your deal." It stepped away deeper into the shadows and chuckled softly. "Oh, to have the four Banes together once more. The fun we'll have. Shall I give you a little taste of how good it can feel to just give in?"

Jimmy fought to breathe normally and get his heartbeat under control. "I've had enough of you," Jimmy growled. "Leave me be."

What in the world had he just agreed to?

A cry sounded from inside the room.

Jimmy dashed back in through the door and found Hope sitting up in bed and Bonnie running around frantically.

"Her water broke," Bonnie said before Jimmy could ask. "Hurry. I need you to get hot water and towels. And call Joaquin. Get us the midwife."

Jimmy hated to leave Hope's side, but as she didn't seem in distress at the moment, he knew he had a few minutes to spare.

His long legs carried him hastily down the stairs and through the back doors to the house at the rear of the inn where the Del Oro clan lived. He knocked assertively and felt awful that he was likely waking the whole family.

A light came on behind the windows and Joaquin was there in an instant.

"Is it time?" he asked with wide eyes.

"It is," Jimmy answered. "Is Miranda able to come? I don't know how much time—"

Miranda appeared behind Joaquin, pulling her coat closed around her with one hand as she hitched up a dark leather bag with her other. "Let us see to your wife."

The men looked at her in surprise, but as she brushed by him, he sensed her otherness. Not like his own, but different. She'd known it was time. She must have, because there was no other explanation as to why she was fully dressed and prepared with all of her necessary items at this hour.

Jimmy thanked Joaquin, who said he and Dolores would be right behind them and would be available in case they needed anything else. He had to hurry to keep up with Miranda's long strides. She moved swiftly, taking the steps at a controlled run, and waited for Jimmy to open the door.

The scene before him frightened him. Bonnie sat behind Hope on the bed, her legs straddling Hope's hips. Hope reclined against Bonnie's chest, her face screwed up in agony. Bonnie wiped at her brow with a wet cloth, but Hope cried out from her pain.

When she could finally catch her breath, Hope reached for Jimmy who remained in the doorway and he hurried to her side.

"Please," she whispered. "Stay with me."

He nodded and pressed a kiss to her forehead. She relaxed the slightest bit and exhaled. Jimmy heard Miranda explaining to her what she was going to do, and the women appeared to be listening intently, but the words were lost on Jimmy.

A buzzing filled Jimmy's ears and his skin began to vibrate. The babies were coming, and with them the rush of energy he'd been anticipating. He didn't want to worry the women, but he could feel the darkness within him rising to the surface to sip from the deliciousness. He should have prepared them for what would happen. Better, he supposed, that they saw him for what he really was. That would take all question away as to what they'd be getting if they remained with him.

Hope pulled Jimmy's hand over to her belly, which was now twitching from the contractions. He gasped when he felt the worry and fear from the babies. They were in pain.

"Miranda," he said quietly, his voice tinged with the otherworldliness that he could not hide. "They are in distress."

The room stilled at his words before chaos erupted. Hope began sobbing and Bonnie growled at Jimmy to do something. Miranda hurried to the door and called for Joaquin to fetch the doctor, "just in case." She also asked for Dolores, and then returned to the foot of the bed.

"Mrs. Manwaring, I need you to open up for me. Let us bring these children into this world."

She murmured in Spanish under her breath the entire time she worked. She set out her instruments and towels before gently lifting the hem of Hope's gown over her bent knees. A sob escaped Bonnie when she saw the blood coating Hope's thighs.

"Do something," she implored of Jimmy, and though he feared what the consequences would be, he nodded.

A flicker of green in the dark, shadowy corner near the door set his blood to boil. He fought back the anger and shame over what he carried inside of him and did the only thing he knew to do. He closed his eyes and reached out with the tendrils from his mind.

Hope slumped in Bonnie's arms and Bonnie started to scream, but Miranda held out her hand.

"No, it is better this way. Let her rest and let us do the work."

Bonnie looked between Jimmy and Miranda fearfully.

"We need you too, Miss Collins. You know what I speak of."

Bonnie's red curls were as wild as her eyes. Her hand trembled as she pushed her hair back and a smear of blood appeared on her cheek. Jimmy groaned and felt the buzzing even more insistent now. He glanced down to see the black lines appearing on his skin where his veins were located and his skin heated to the point where he knew the flames would erupt any moment and probably scare the daylights out of the women.

"I've relaxed her and I can ease the babies, but you and Miranda need to coax them out," Jimmy said.

11
─────────

Bonnie gasped at Jimmy's words. She'd seen what he truly was when she'd touched him before, but experiencing it in the flesh was overwhelming to say the least.

"Jimmy! Your eyes."

He looked away and growled. "Don't look at me. Just do what Miranda says."

Bonnie swallowed hard and locked on Miranda. She'd have to focus on the midwife or she'd lose her nerve.

"Miss Collins, I know you have a bit of the Sight. I need you to focus for me. For Mrs. Manwaring. Concentrate on giving her the energy she's going to need."

"But I don't know how to do that," Bonnie cried. A dim green light came from Jimmy's direction, but she refused to look. "Tell me what to do."

Miranda regarded her for a moment and then nodded. "Touch my hand. You'll know what to do."

Bonnie leaned forward and touched the woman's outstretched hand.

Flashes.

Cells.

Arteries.

Muscles.

Womb.

Fingers and toes.

Heartbeats. Erratic.

Concentrate.

Bonnie inhaled deeply and on her exhale, she imagined the babies moving, being moved.

Concentrate.

"Come to me, little ones," she purred. In her mind's eye, she saw the flashes of green light around her, illuminating the scene on the bed. Miranda's voice continued on, her words incomprehensible, but their meaning she felt deep in her bones.

Concentrate.

She inhaled once more and her exhale acted as a force against Bonnie's own womb and Hope's at the same time, which contracted and forced the first baby's head to emerge.

"She's crowning," Miranda said urgently. "Again, Miss Collins."

Bonnie inhaled, deeper than before, and blew out her breath with a huff, her lungs burning with the effort.

A moment later an infant's cry echoed in the dark room. Bonnie opened her eyes to see Mrs. Del Oro take one of the twins from Miranda, who hurriedly returned to Hope.

"Miss Collins! Again!" she cried.

Bonnie was panting from the strain, but she repeated her breathing and this time as the air was forced out, she shouted, beginning to feel weak and tired and wishing she could give up. It was so difficult to hold up her head even.

"She's crowning. More, Miss Collins. Miss Johnson needs you to do what she cannot."

Bonnie nodded. She caressed Hope's forehead and worried at the state of her friend.

"I love you, baby," she whispered. She gathered up as much energy as she could and sucked in as much oxygen as her body could take. When she blew it out, the force was enough to force the baby's head and shoulders to be free.

"He's not breathing," Miranda said as she cleaned off the babe with a towel. She prayed over him in Spanish, or at least that's what Bonnie assumed she was doing. Her limbs were dead weight, and she slumped back against the bars of the bed frame. Her belly ached and between her legs...well, she may not have given birth herself, but her body didn't know that.

Miranda was at her side, holding the child out to her.

"Once more. For the child. You can do it, Miss Collins."

Bonnie blinked back tears and somehow found the strength to sit up and take the child into her arms. He was so still.

"No," she whispered. "No, sweet boy. You need to breathe for your mama. Breathe for her. Breathe for me." Bonnie gathered in one last shaky breath, but this time when she exhaled, she blew gently into the child's face, willing her energy to flow into him and bring him back from the brink of death. She hugged him to her chest and her tears fell on his face.

He stirred but did not yet breathe.

"Again."

The eerie voice did not come from Miranda.

She allowed herself to look in Jimmy's direction and immediately understood why he'd said to look away.

Jimmy's eyes glowed green and there was an aura about him that swirled in the same green hue. The black lines running through his skin throbbed as though with his heartbeat. He'd kept his hands on Hope's belly the entire time until the babies were both out. Now, he implored Bonnie to do what she must.

"I can't," she said, feeling the last of her energy leaving her. Sobs wracked her body and though the child squirmed, he'd yet to breathe. "I can't."

Jimmy's hand shot out and grabbed her arm. Her skin burned with the contact and she gasped.

"*Again!*"

Bonnie had only enough energy to take in a weak breath and blow it into the child's face.

As the lights dimmed around her, Bonnie felt the child removed from her arms just as a piercing, shrill cry emanated from his tiny body. It wasn't a cry of announcement. It was a shout of defiance. A darkness clouded Bonnie's awareness just as she fell to the side and lost consciousness.

12

Hope was stunned at the beauty before her.

Somehow, despite her sins and misdeeds in this life, she'd been given the two most perfect babies of all time.

The girl child was all round cheeks, round belly, and cute pudgy toes.

The boy child already had little muscles, which he flexed with every movement, making his demanding presence known.

While the girl's features were soft and peaceful, the boy's face remained almost constantly in what she could only describe as a scowl. He fussed and fussed and never seemed to get his fill from her breast. It seemed all she'd done for the past three days was eat and feed them.

Luckily, she had Jimmy to dote on her, and though he seemed worried over her and the children, he couldn't help but touch them every chance he got and smiled while he did it. He'd remained by her side through most of the time, and she found she craved his presence almost like she thought the children had when in the womb. Jimmy was magic. That had to be it. He didn't need to do or say anything, he just put her at ease in a way she'd never experienced, not even with Bonnie.

Hope remembered nothing of the night she delivered the twins other than falling asleep in bed wedged between Jimmy and Bonnie, their bodies pressed against hers to provide comfort and security. She'd let her thoughts wander to what the future held for the three of them and hoped that whatever may come of their time together, there were plenty more nights like this. The next thing she knew, she was waking up to be handed these two perfect bundles.

Miranda and Dolores were in a constant state of motion in their room, changing the babies, bringing her food, cleaning up after all of them. Miranda had even helped her bathe after she'd woken up and fed the babies for the first time and she'd been surprised to find she wasn't very sore, just a bit more uncomfortable than usual. She asked Miranda if that was normal.

Miranda winked. "It is when I deliver the babies. I have been well trained by the women in my family. For generations we have brought healthy, strong children into this world, and we always take care of the mothers."

Hope smiled and a hand instinctively went to her belly, which was gone. It wasn't exactly flat as it had been before the babies, but she didn't mind. The marks on her skin and the bit of extra padding would always remind her of the feeling she'd had of them moving within her. She just hoped Bonnie still thought she was beautiful like she always said. She knew Jimmy did. He couldn't help his frequent appreciative glances and gazes in her direction. But Bonnie...

All Jimmy would tell her was that the delivery took a lot out of Bonnie and he'd put her to rest in the room next door so she could regain her strength before returning to Hope's side. That hadn't set too well with Hope, but she trusted him after she'd seen with her own eyes that Bonnie was resting next door. She knew, however, that they weren't telling her everything. Her focus had to be on the babies now. She would trust that Jimmy was taking care of Bonnie like he said.

That night after Miranda and Dolores said their goodnights, Hope walked them to the door and locked it behind them. She smiled as she watched Jimmy cooing to the babies while rocking them in the large wooden rocker Joaquin had brought them this afternoon. Jimmy was in just his undershirt and had a baby in each arm, speaking softly to each of them and singing a gentle lullaby. They were so serene there in his arms, Hope could only shake her head remembering just how difficult they'd both been earlier when Dolores taught her how to change their diapers and swaddle them.

"I suppose we should be naming them soon," Hope said, moving to his side.

Jimmy glanced up at her and smiled wider than she'd ever seen and for a moment, she was angry on his behalf that he'd never had his chance to be a father. She couldn't think of a more deserving man, not even Daddy.

"They'll make their names known soon enough," Jimmy said, leaning down to rub his nose across the top of the little girl's head. "Can you believe how amazing they are? I've never smelled a more heavenly scent in my life. And did you see her toes? How pudgy they are! And this little man right here, so strong already—"

"Jimmy, I want them to have your name." She'd decided right there on the spot.

Jimmy frowned up at her. She cut him off as he started to speak.

"Miranda called me Mrs. Manwaring. Did you tell her we were married?"

Jimmy sighed and rested his head against the back of the chair with his eyes closed.

"Joaquin knows the truth. He actually suggested it to avoid any issues. He wrote it in the register, so Miranda must have seen it. I'm sorry…"

Hope sat on the trunk at the foot of the bed and smiled at him. "Don't be sorry. I can never thank you enough for taking care of us, of them. For saving my life. There's no way for me to ever repay your kindness. But I can do this for you. I don't expect you to marry me—"

"Hope—"

"Let me get this out. Please. I know they are another man's children, a man that no longer breathes. I know I have no right to ask, and I would never assume you would support us—"

Jimmy stood from the chair and carefully walked over to the bassinet the Del Oros had brought for them to use. He placed the bundles side by side and made sure they were settled before turning back to Hope. He approached her slowly and lowered himself to one knee before her.

"Hope, don't answer me yet, because there is another person we must take into consideration. I would very, *very* much like to marry you and to raise these children as their father."

Hope started to speak, but Jimmy shook his head.

"Please let *me* finish. When I first felt them at the saloon, they were so familiar to me, and for some reason I don't rightly understand, they felt like mine, like they were meant for me. It might sound crazy, but I can't help but think my wife had a hand in bringing us together from the afterlife. She made me promise on her deathbed that I would protect them and have hope." He took her hands in his. "I would never come between you and Bonnie, but I would lay down my life for these children, and I would very much like to have you however you have room for me in your heart, Hope."

Hope's hand flew to her cheek and she felt the heat coming off of her skin. Jimmy Manwaring, mysterious piano player, hotel purveyor, and reluctant hero, wanted to make her his wife. He was strikingly handsome, cautious, intelligent, and possessed a wry sense of humor that kept Hope grounded and positive. She would be crazy to say no. She desperately wanted what he was offering.

"But what about Bonnie?" she asked what she knew they were both thinking.

Jimmy moved closer and rested one hand on her thigh, the other he reached up to smooth back her unruly hair.

"I would never act without her acceptance, and I would very much like her to continue to be a part of us. This...family...It's all of us." He closed his eyes for a moment and took in a deep breath. "I will wait for your answer until you discuss it with her. But Hope," he said, moving closer still, until his face was mere inches away from hers. "I have very strong feelings for you that are above and beyond your children. I love them with all of my being, but their mother holds a very big piece of my heart in her hands. Please consider my request."

He stood only tall enough to place a gentle kiss on her lips, and with his kiss, she felt a sting she wouldn't necessarily consider painful. Almost like when a person touches another and that little spark happens that zaps them both. The way Jimmy touched his lips as he stood made her think he felt it too.

"I'm going to go check on Bonnie. Miranda's mother Carmen has been staying with her when I am with you. I'll give you time to prepare for bed before I return."

Hope nodded. She stood and swayed a bit, her body still not completely recovered. Jimmy caught her weight against his body with a soft grunt. His hands gripped her upper arms gentle but firm.

"Are you well?" Jimmy asked, rubbing his thumbs along her skin. Hope thought for sure she must be on fire, his touch like a brand.

"I am," she said, pushing up onto her tiptoes. She placed a kiss on his bottom lip that appeared to startle him as his grip tightened. "May I go with you to see Bonnie? I'm worried about her."

Jimmy nodded. He pulled out a key from his pocket and handed it to her. "I will stay with the children then," he said, returning to the rocking chair.

"Thank you," she said, giving him a parting smile. "I won't be long."

He smiled at her as he rested his hands on his stomach. His eyelids drooped low over his eyes, creating a look that was either incredibly sleepy or incredibly aroused. Which one was true for him, Hope could only guess.

"Take your time," he said with a smile. "I'll tend to the beasts. Who probably *will* need to have names soon. Miranda filled out their birth certificates and will register them for us as soon as we put in those important details." He grinned and Hope loved the way his lips curled up on one side. She loved many things about him. She might even love *him*.

Hope scooted out of the door, intending to check on Bonnie, and then return to Jimmy's soothing presence. She composed herself in the hallway and used the key to open the door.

Carmen sat up in the chair next to the bed and smiled at her. She only spoke Spanish, so Hope had been unable to communicate with her, but she said thank you and the tiny woman bowed her head and left the room.

Bonnie lay restless in the bed. Her cheeks were flushed and the sheets were rumpled all around her. Sweat glistened on her brow and her hair was damp with it as well. Hope sat on the side of the bed and took Bonnie's hand in hers.

Bonnie's eyes opened slowly and a relieved smile graced her face.

"I've missed you."

"I'm sorry," Hope said. "I saw you shortly after, but I haven't been able to get up and around much until today. Jimmy is with the babies."

Bonnie closed her eyes and nodded. "He loves those children. He's told me so much about them. I didn't know there was so much to tell about a baby, but he's rambled on about their toes, their hands, the way they eat, how much they eat, how they look at their mama." She smiled and opened her eyes, giving Hope's hand a weak squeeze.

Hope worried that her friend was in such a state. "I don't remember what happened. Any of it after my water broke. What happened to you? Why are you so ill?"

Bonnie licked her lips and reached for her glass of water. Hope got there first and held it to her parched lips. Bonnie sipped and then lay back, her eyes drifting shut once more.

"There were complications," she said. "Jimmy and I helped deliver the babies. Miranda told us what to do and we did it."

Hope frowned. "That doesn't tell me why you are so ill."

Bonnie sighed. "I don't know what to tell you. I don't really understand it myself."

Hope waited impatiently as Bonnie tried to push herself up to a sitting position. Hope leaned forward to help her adjust the pillows and then took her hand once more.

"Try," Hope urged.

Bonnie took another sip of water and attempted to smooth back her frizzy curls. "You know how I know things? How sometimes I touch people and I See?"

Hope nodded, a chill running through her as she feared what Bonnie would say next.

"Miranda is like that, too. Sort of. And you know Jimmy is...other. I can't explain it, but somehow whatever it is that makes *me* like them, I used it to help you push them babies out." Bonnie leaned forward suddenly. "Oh Hope, don't cry. We didn't do no harm to them! I swear, I'd die before I ever let anyone hurt you. But we were gonna lose you and the twins if we didn't."

Hope went into Bonnie's arms and wept. They slid down together on the bed, and Bonnie held her weakly as she cried.

"I'm so sorry I wasn't strong enough. I hate it that I hurt you."

Bonnie shushed her. "You didn't hurt me none. I told you I'd take care of you, protect you."

Bonnie smiled and Hope's tears turned to giggles. "You should hear that man carry on. Tell me, love. Are they as beautiful as we thought they would be?"

"More. Girlie is so soft and cuddly, and Big Boy is so strong and willful. I don't know what I would do without you and Jimmy. I don't think I could handle this on my own."

Bonnie grazed Hope's cheek with her thumb. "You could, but you don't ever have to."

Hope placed her hand over Bonnie's. "I don't want to, but I do want something and I don't know how you're going to feel about it."

Bonnie tilted her head to the side and sighed. "He's asked you to marry him."

"Yes. How did you know?"

"I figured he would once they came. One look at those beauties and he would be a goner."

Hope laughed and pulled Bonnie closer. Without her belly in the way, they fit so well together, just like they had in the beginning when she'd been on the run and so afraid. She never thought she'd get away from her husband, and after his accidental death, she thought she'd never be safe from the law. She hadn't thought about it in some time, not since Jimmy'd taken them in, but then Charlie's death... Would they ever be able to live a peaceful life?

"He says he would never act without your acceptance, and I know he wants you to be with us. He cares about you very much."

Bonnie leaned down to kiss Hope's neck. "I know he does. He's become important to all of us, and while I know he understands how I feel about you and how I feel about men, I can't help but worry what my part will be in all of this."

"Bonnie, I love you. I won't ever leave you. But I love him, too, and the babies love him, I can tell. I don't know how to make this all work."

Bonnie shrugged. "You marry him. We stay together. It's that simple. He can't legally marry us both, but we're going to be a family. That's what he wants, that's what I want. For sure it's what them babies want!"

Hope kissed Bonnie gently and then looked into her lover's eyes. "Are you well? Have you recovered?"

Bonnie smiled. "I have. My fever broke this afternoon. I'm just tired and I'd really like a bath."

Hope stood from the bed. "Then let me help you. I want you to come back to our room, our bed. Tonight. I want to sleep beside you. Both of you." She held out a hand to Bonnie and helped her climb from the bed.

WHEN BONNIE and Hope entered the room, they found Jimmy asleep in the rocker while the babies slept soundly together in their bassinet. Bonnie teared up at the sight of the babes and smiled at Hope. Then they quietly made their way to the bathroom where Hope helped Bonnie bathe, relishing the switch of roles.

"Now I get to take care of you," she murmured, kissing Bonnie's shoulder.

Hope loved Bonnie's body, how different it felt from her own, and she couldn't wait until they could pleasure each other again, which led to thoughts of Jimmy. What would it be like to have him in their bed? Would Bonnie object? Hope had already made it clear that she wanted the three of them to share their bed, but what that meant for sure, she didn't know.

The women crawled into bed and sighed with relief at being skin to skin once again and they spent several moments locked in an embrace and kissing each other deeply.

The rocking chair creaked, and Hope glanced over to see Jimmy watching them. She smiled and gestured for him to join them. Jimmy shook his head but kept watching.

Bonnie looked between the two of them and smiled. "He won't join us until he's made you his bride, isn't that right Jimmy?"

Jimmy cleared his throat and shook his head but didn't speak.

The women watched him as he appeared to be fighting for control over his emotions. He gripped the armrests of the chair so hard it creaked ominously.

"Until then you're just going to watch us, aren't you Jimmy?" Bonnie asked with a laugh.

A flash of green light from his eyes let Hope know they'd provoked him, and she paused for a moment, afraid Bonnie had taken their game too far, but then she watched in awe as Jimmy slid one of his large hands with the long fingers down his chest and stomach. He unbuttoned his trousers and slid his hand below the fabric and out of Hope's sight. His arm muscles flexed in the moonlight as he began to pleasure himself and the sight of his movements caused her to ache at the juncture of her thighs, reminding her that soon she would be healed...and she would be ready for him. She only hoped it would be soon. She turned to look at Bonnie, the woman who'd been so good to her, and it occurred to her that she could provide pleasure to both of her loves.

Hope drew back the blankets and pulled the sheers open around the bed, giving Jimmy a clear view of their naked bodies together. Bonnie watched her with an amused grin on her face. Hope wanted to replace her amusement with desire. She crawled on her hands and knees to the foot of the bed, never losing eye contact with Bonnie.

She glanced over her shoulder to hear Jimmy groan, his hand still moving beneath his trousers.

Hope placed her hands on Bonnie's legs and pushed them gently apart. Bonnie's eyes went wide and her smile slipped a little. Hope pressed kisses against the insides of Bonnie's calves, knees, and thighs as she slithered closer to Bonnie's core. She ran her fingernails gently through the red curls she found there and Bonnie squirmed under her touch.

Hope was determined to show Bonnie just how much she loved her and appreciated all she'd done for her by reciprocating the gentle touch Bonnie'd given to her when they'd become lovers. She'd given Hope's body such an overwhelming pleasure, such ecstasy. Hope used her fingers and tongue to make Bonnie crazy with lust, loving every cry from her mouth. Bonnie thrashed beneath Hope's ministrations until her torso bowed up from the bed, her head thrown back in a silent scream. She trembled as her body contracted and then she collapsed back onto the pillows laughing and gasping for air.

Hope, still on her knees, turned to look over her shoulder at Jimmy. The green light still emanated from his eyes, and along his forearm, she swore she saw marks on his skin that she'd never seen before. He moaned softly and then his body tensed up. He shuddered and exhaled harshly. When he opened his eyes, the green hue was gone. His lip twitched up at the corner and Hope could tell he was pleased. She wondered at his reactions and thought how incredible it was that she'd given him such pleasure without even touching him. What would it be like when she lay with him as his wife?

Jimmy stood and entered the bathroom, his gaze traveling over the naked women as he passed. Bonnie giggled and reached out a hand to touch his arm. Jimmy shook his head and chuckled.

"What has gotten into my little Hope?" Bonnie asked, pulling Hope tighter against her.

Hope shrugged. "I just wanted to make you feel good. Both of you. I know I like it when you do that to me. I never had the chance to do it to you before, and I wanted to."

Bonnie grazed her nails along Hope's shoulder. "Well, feel free to practice anytime. That was amazing." Bonnie kissed her deeply, their tongues dancing together. "I look forward to returning the favor when you've healed."

Hope sighed. "And I look forward to receiving."

Jimmy came out of the bathroom wrapped in a bathrobe and paused next to the bassinet. "They'll probably want to eat soon," he said, his voice sounding gravelly. "I'll wait up—"

"Jimmy, please," Hope said, reaching for him. "Come lay with us. You haven't rested, really rested, in so long."

Either he was too tired to resist, or he'd accepted that he was truly wanted. He walked slowly around to Hope's side of the bed and stood there, unsure. Hope lifted up the covers for him to join them and he sighed. He kept his robe on, but he slid in next to the Hope and rolled onto his side. He gazed at Hope with his green eyes, as if looking for permission.

Hope rolled to face him and only hesitated briefly before she pressed her lips to his. Startled, he pulled back. He looked past Hope as though asking permission from Bonnie. Bonnie curled up against her back and lightly drag her nails over Hope's hip before she rested her chin on Hope's shoulder.

"You can do whatever you want as long as I get to watch this time."

Jimmy's eyes widened in surprise.

Hope couldn't help but giggle at his reaction. She pressed a hand to his cheek. "I want to take care of you."

Jimmy placed his hand over hers and turned to kiss her palm. When he looked back at her, his gaze was so serious.

"You already have."

13

Jimmy woke the next morning disoriented. Instead of the ceiling over the couch, the pattern of the fabric on the canopy greeted him. Instead of being sore and stiff, he was well rested. Well, he was stiff, but that was an entirely different matter. To his right lay Bonnie on her stomach sleeping soundly. Cooing sounds brought his attention to the bassinet where Hope sat rocking her son and nursing him.

Her son. *His* son. Could he be? The children had called to him from her womb. That had to mean something. He'd been around pregnant women before and not had the same experience. There was something special about the twins, that he knew. Just being near them, holding them, soothed his weary soul and made the darkness a little easier to fight back.

Would Hope marry him? Would the world accept the children as his? He wasn't so much a fool to think he wouldn't run into bigotry wherever they went, but might they also find acceptance? He wanted to marry her as soon as possible, if she and Bonnie consented, and had already asked Joaquin to find him an official who would perform the civil ceremony. They would make Bonnie godmother to the children, and he would be sure she knew she was part of their covenant. It could be done. His people in the Utah Territory believed in plural wives all those years ago. He'd even known families with plural wives as a young man. It was a common practice in the early years of the settlement. The church banned the practice before the turn of the century under pressure from the government, understandably, as the practice had led to the abuse of young women. Jimmy tried not judge the families who practiced polygamy as long as no one was hurt or unable to give their consent. Who was he to judge anyone after what he'd been party to in the desert?

And what he was still party to. He wondered if he should tell the women about his visitor from the night of the children's birth and the promise he'd made to the creature. He needed to take his new family to Reno and reunite with his brothers. The thought of seeing Lionel and William again turned his stomach. Nathaniel...he still had hope that someday they could be brothers again, assuming the spark of humanity he himself clung to was still present inside his dearest brother. The other two he'd have to form a working relationship with, one that did not involve being an accomplice in any of their dark arts. And his bride and partner would never receive rings of silver, or any cursed jewelry for that matter, that would bind them to him or the family. He would keep Hope, Bonnie, and the children safe, or he would leave Reno forever and pray that he could conquer the creature on his own.

"I swear I smell smoke coming from over there," Hope said quietly from her chair.

Jimmy sat up and grinned at her. He'd managed to lose his bathrobe sometime in the night and realized he was only wearing his underwear, that he'd slept with the women nearly naked. For some reason that bothered him, though he thought it silly to be worried about such things. He'd had carnal knowledge of women since his Julianna passed away, but it had always been out of necessity, and he'd rarely disrobed. It felt too intimate an act. He'd wanted to be naked with Hope, though, and damn him for it. He wanted to do right by her, not take further advantage of her.

"Smoke?"

"You're thinking pretty hard. Would you mind taking little man so I can feed his sister?"

Jimmy cursed to himself for leaving her on her own with the babies. "I'm sorry, Hope. I wish you would have woken me. I should be helping you."

She laughed at him and pulled her sleeping boy from her nipple and put him to her shoulder to burp him. "We were just fine. His sister loves her sleep."

Jimmy reached for the robe on the floor and hurriedly put it on, blushing at the sound of her laughter. He walked to her side and gently took the boy from her arms. The little man's arms and legs pumped underneath his blanket as Jimmy gently placed him on his shoulder. He'd gotten the hang of the whole after-meal routine and enjoyed spending the time with the baby.

Jimmy watched Hope expertly scoop up her daughter from the bassinet where she was just starting to fuss. She sat down in the rocker and placed the child to her breast. The little angel began nursing lazily, not desperate like her brother.

"How long have you been up?" Jimmy asked her.

"Not long. Did you sleep well?"

He really had. He nodded to her and moved the little man to rest on his tummy on his forearm. He quieted down and began to relax.

"I can't believe how quickly you get him to stop fussing," she remarked.

"Good morning," Jimmy heard from behind him just as Bonnie placed her hands on his shoulders and kissed him on the cheek. She leaned over to pat the little man on his back. "How are our precious angels this morning?"

Hope smiled at her and Jimmy tried to contain his shock that Bonnie was being affectionate with him. He glanced at her as she climbed off the bed and stretched.

"How about I go down and have Joaquin bring up breakfast?" Bonnie asked them. Jimmy frowned at her but she rolled her eyes at him. "We're safe here, Jimmy. And I need to get out of this room!"

Jimmy looked down at the baby. "We're leaving soon," he said, not making eye contact.

Hope frowned and shifted the baby girl to the other breast. "What do you mean? Where will we go?"

"Reno."

Bonnie froze where she'd been putting on her dress. "Reno? You can't be serious."

Jimmy shot her a stern look, which she answered with a frown. She planted her fists on her hips, and it became very clear to Hope that they were having a silent conversation, one that Bonnie was very unhappy about.

"I have no choice, Bonnie. I—"

"Made a promise! To your wife. You're really going to bring the babies into that world?"

"They will be safe, I promise you."

"Jimmy?" Hope needed to know what was going on.

Jimmy was torn. He knew what he needed to do, felt confident that he could keep them safe.

There was a knock on the door. The women hurried to dress and Jimmy put on his pants before opening the door.

Joaquin stood there with trays of food. "I brought breakfast. And some news."

His solemn expression concerned Jimmy. He helped Joaquin set the trays down and left the women without a word to follow Joaquin out the door. He followed the shorter man down the steps to his office where Joaquin gestured for him to enter, and then he closed the door.

"I did some checking for you and we have a problem."

Jimmy had asked Joaquin to find a justice of the peace who would marry he and Hope, assuming she and Bonnie agreed. He knew it was premature, but he wanted to have everything lined up.

Jimmy crossed his arms over his chest. "Tell me."

Joaquin sighed. "I had a feeling this might be an issue, but I asked anyway. Reverend Olsen, the justice of the peace here in Grass Valley, he will not agree to perform the ceremony. He reminded me that he'd wed my son Ramon to his bride as a favor to me, she was a

Caucasian girl from the next town, but that there are laws against this."

Jimmy frowned. "What do you mean?"

"It is against California law for a white person to marry someone who is not white."

Joaquin looked down at his feet, obviously ashamed about the subject of their conversation.

Jimmy cursed under his breath. "Well, we'll have to wait until we get to Reno—"

"It is against the law there as well," he said quietly.

Jimmy felt his anger surge and he took a few breaths to calm himself. There was no need ruining his friendship with Joaquin Del Oro over things out of both of their control.

"It might be against the law, but in Reno, my brothers *are* the law. As much as I hate to be beholden to them, in this case I just might have to. I will not have those children called bastards. I will be their father, and their mother will be my wife. It must be this way. No one is going to stand in my way."

A slow smile spread across Joaquin's lips. He reached in a cabinet behind him and pulled out two glasses and a carafe of amber liquid. "Then we shall toast to the health of your new family, my old friend. I want to share in your happiness."

Jimmy relaxed a little. Now that events were set in motion, there was really nothing else to do. They would go to Reno, Lionel would marry he and Hope, and the children would have his name.

Joaquin slid a glass his way and they clinked them together. "Salud, mi hermano," Joaquin said.

"To the health of you and yours. I cannot thank you enough. I plan to leave Miranda a hefty sum in payment, but what can I do for you?"

Joaquin swirled the liquid around in his glass. "You have always assured me that if I am in need, I can call on you. My wife and I have all we need here. Business is good, the hotel is very successful, and our children and grandchildren are happy and healthy. But I do have a favor to ask that will benefit us both."

"Anything. You know that."

Joaquin took another drink. "My brother recently had some trouble in his family in Mexico. My sister Carmen—Miranda's mother—and my brother, Eduardo, are twins. They are both *brujas*. Eduardo's sons, Canneo and Danaá, both are very strong. People in town, they have always suspected our family. It has become dangerous for Eduardo's sons to stay there, so he sent them to me."

"And how can I help?"

Joaquin swirled the drink in his glass. "Your family is in need of protection. My family is in need of discretion. Having this many *brujas* in our town here is a problem. People are already unhappy about my family and our influence in this town, and in the past, the Del Oro's have faced challenges as a result. I would very much like for you to take my nephews with you to Reno."

Jimmy offered his hand and the two men shook. "We are friends, brothers. What brought us together may have been nefarious, but our bond is true. You can always count on me."

They hugged with lots of backslapping and had a couple more drinks together, toasting the health of the babies, safe travels, and a good reception from his brothers. Joaquin knew how Jimmy had left things with them, and he understood how difficult returning would be. Only this time, Jimmy understood his powers, had mastered them to a point he did not fear a confrontation. Lionel had his beliefs, no matter how twisted they were, and William had brawn, but Jimmy did not fear either of those any longer. And wealth? Jimmy had plenty. If they refused his request that Lionel marry him and Hope, he had no trouble resorting to using his influence to find someone who would, but he didn't want to resort to that. There would be no question if Lionel wed them. He had that much power. Jimmy's main concern was keeping their influence from his women and his children. *His*.

Jimmy returned to the room, ready to explain himself. What he wasn't ready for was the jolt to his heart at the sight of his family sitting together, waiting for him with eager faces. He had a huge responsibility here, one he'd wanted for so long. It just hadn't come to him the way he'd imagined it would.

Bonnie's determined gaze caught his eye.

"When do we leave?"

14

Hope had appreciated the time they'd had in Grass Valley, but she understood they needed to leave before the roads and rails became impassable with the snow. She remembered how frightening their passage had been on the train over the majestic Sierra Nevada mountains, and hadn't been looking forward to doing it again, but she trusted Jimmy.

On a cold October morning, late in the month, they were ready to leave the hotel and move on to the next phase of their lives together. She tried not to be afraid of what Reno held for them. Bonnie and Jimmy had explained that they would be going to be with his brothers, who he'd been estranged from for many years, but he told her he would tell her the rest after they arrived.

"All you need to know is that neither of you, nor the children are ever to be left alone with them. And don't accept any gifts from them."

"All right," Hope answered, still puzzled.

He and Bonnie had spoken in whispers when they thought she was sleeping, and it seemed as though he were preparing her for battle. She'd also gone off with Miranda for several hours and came back excited about something she said she couldn't rightly explain.

Jimmy seemed even more tense than usual, unless he was holding the babies. Then he melted like snow on a hot spring day. She knew the children were lucky to have him. So were she and Bonnie. He'd become their rock, and she was grateful for it. But was that enough to keep them safe?

A knock on the door sounded and Jimmy stood to answer. Outside Joaquin stood with two young men.

"Joaquin," Jimmy said, a puzzled expression on his face.

"Delbert has prepared the car to take you to the train, but I have something I want to give you."

Jimmy held the door open and the three men came in. The two unknown men were young, perhaps still in their teens, but they were fierce. There was definitely a resemblance between them and Joaquin.

"These are my nephews from Mexico, Canneo and Danaá. They were sent here by their mother, my sister, because they are like us. They needed training. It is dangerous for them to remain at home, but they are warriors. They will protect the women and children if something is to happen to you, my friend."

Jimmy seemed to size them up, to take their measure. Hope noticed his lip twitch just as he shook hands with both of them. The young men nodded and offered a similarly small smile of acknowledgment.

"They understand English?"

Joaquin nodded and the young men smiled. "I have taught them the ways of your people. They will be great assets to you on this journey."

Jimmy rested his hands on his hips. "Boys, I can't tell you what type of reception we will have from my brothers and their followers. My brothers are very powerful. They have the ability to influence people."

"Not us," Canneo said. "We can fight it."

Danaá nodded.

Jimmy seemed to be testing them. A staring contest between the three of them went on for some time. Hope wondered what he was doing. No one moved. There may have been a twitch in Canneo's knee after several minutes, but the two young men stood solid, neither bending to Jimmy's will.

Jimmy smiled. "It's a start." He turned to Joaquin and took his hand. "I cannot thank you enough, my friend, for your hospitality, your protection...And please tell your women we appreciate all of their help. I swear, I shall make this up to you."

Joaquin waved away Jimmy's sentiment. "It is how we do, yes? We watch out for each other."

"And thank God for that."

Hope tried not to be overwhelmed by all of this. She needed to trust Jimmy that they were doing the right thing.

THE JOURNEY by train to Reno was long, but she and the babies were able to rest, thanks to Jimmy and Bonnie. Jimmy was quiet for most of the way. He seemed preoccupied. After several hours, she stood to stretch her legs.

"Are you alright?" he asked her.

"Walk with me," she said. "I need to move and I'd love a cup of coffee."

It was late at night and most of the passengers were sleeping. Bonnie was resting near the babies in their private car, and Canneo and Danaá stood watch outside.

"The bar car may still be open," Jimmy said, standing and holding out a hand to her.

Hope accepted it and felt a little thrill to be standing so close to him. Since the night he'd slept beside her, he'd been somewhat distant. She knew he'd enjoyed her kiss, that he desired her, but he was holding back.

They moved through the train to the bar car and sure enough, the bartender was still cleaning up after a long night. Two couples sat at the far end of the car. Jimmy asked the man for two coffees and he nodded in agreement. Jimmy led her over to a booth and held her hand as she slid onto the bench seat. He sat across from her and thanked the bar man for their coffees.

"Thank you," Hope said, sipping her coffee and sighing happily. "This is delicious."

"You are so beautiful," Jimmy said, his cheeks reddening. Perhaps he hadn't meant to say that out loud?

"As are you to me," she answered, looking down at her hands with a shy smile. "I can't thank you—"

"You don't ever need to thank me. It is *I* who should thank you for believing me when I told you why I'd been there for you, for allowing me to share in the joy of your children—"

"*Our* children, Jimmy. I want you to be their father. I know it's not the same as having your own blood, but they want you. I want you."

Jimmy cleared his throat. "Then you'll consent to be my wife? We can be married when we arrive?"

"I would like that very much."

Jimmy smiled, finally a real smile. He reached tentatively across the table and took her hand. Hope loved the way his fingers, so strong and soft, intertwined with hers. She wished she had nice, ladylike fingers like some of the fancy women she'd known in her life. At one point her hands were nice, not dry and brittle from washing dishes. She hated for her hands to be abrasive on the skin of her babes, but she'd had to work hard to ensure they were provided for. Now? Could she really hope that Jimmy would—

"I will take care of you, Hope. You, the babies, and Bonnie, I swear this to you. I know the circumstances of our meeting were not ideal. I've not been able to court you as I would like, but I swear to you, Hope—"

"Jimmy, you don't have to—"

"But I do, Hope. How I feel, what I want...Even if my wife would never have spoken the words, I would still want you the way that I do."

Hope felt her skin heating from his touch, and it traveled up her arm to curve around her face before drifting down her throat to her chest, where it settled in the place she imagined her heart resided. She felt heat, and she felt Jimmy.

"Tell me about Jonah," she said.

The warmth emanating from him evaporated.

"I've heard Bonnie use that name, and Joaquin..."

"I've not gone by that name since my wife died long ago. I buried Jonah Bane in the ashes with her body."

Hope waited, hating to put him through this, but needing answers.

He took another drink of his coffee and sighed. "Jonah and his three brothers traveled from Utah Territory on a mission from God to Nevada Territory in 1860. They were called there to create a new civilization and do God's work." He ran his finger around the rim of the cup, refusing to look at her.

"And what happened then?"

He looked up and his mournful gaze penetrated her.

"It was not God's work. It was never God. Something evil was at work, and that evil cast its spell over Jonah and his brothers. Jonah was able to escape, with his lovely bride, but that evil will always be a part of him."

"Something tells me you've become its master."

Jimmy exhaled harshly. "Most of the time. It's taken me years, but I have managed to keep it at bay. At the same time, I am a slave to its power. I need to feed it, otherwise it weakens me, and in my weak state I know I am no longer in control."

"The saloon, the hotel...the babies?"

"All part of what I need to survive. I do no harm, but I *need*...yes." He leaned back against the booth and spread his long arms over the back, gazing out the window. "I suppose I should be prepared to become Jonah once more. My brothers will likely call me that, anyway. I have no idea whether or not they have taken on other names, or if they've used their influence to keep the townspeople of Reno in the dark about their past."

Hope nodded and glanced around the bar car. They were alone

save the bartender. She leaned forward, placing her elbows on the table.

"Does it make a difference, with your *needs*, if you are a participant rather than just a witness?"

Jimmy's eyes bugged out. It was his turn to glance around. "Are we really having this conversation?"

Hope shrugged. "Might as well. There's no use avoiding it. If I'm going to be your wife, I want to know what you need. You've taken care of us so well...I want to be a good wife to you."

Jimmy cocked his head to one side and frowned. "You were a good wife before."

Hope sat back so quickly the air whooshed out of her lungs. She didn't know what to say to that. Did he know?

"I did the best I could with what I had."

"You deserved better," he said, his voice taking on a deeper, almost ethereal tone. It startled Hope, but it was over before she knew it. She thought perhaps she'd imagined it.

"I *found* better."

"Hope...you know I'm not an ordinary man," he said not as a question but as an assumption.

"I do." She reached for his hand again. "I'm not afraid."

Her answer didn't placate him. He seemed agitated, as though he wanted to say more, but feared the repercussions.

"Yes, it makes a difference," he finally said, and his words burned right through her. She fidgeted in her seat.

"Miranda said I should wait until the next full moon, then it will have been long enough for my body to heal."

Jimmy's cheeks flushed and she swore she saw a faint green light come from his eyes. It faded quickly and Jimmy cleared his throat, leaning forward on his elbows on the table.

"That doesn't have to be part of this. Making you my wife...I don't expect things. I'd never—"

"It's all right, Jimmy. I know there is more about you I don't know, more that is keeping you from accepting that I desire you. You feel you need absolution. You'll tell me when the time is right. I trust you to keep the babies and Bonnie and I safe. That's all I need for now."

His eyes were so deep green, the sadness in them was like an endless sea of mourning. How much he'd lost! Hope was more determined than ever to bring him happiness.

They finished their coffee and other than playing with each other's fingers on the table, smiling shyly at each other, they'd fallen quiet. Hope yawned and that was Jimmy's signal to take her back to their car.

"You need rest. I want you fully aware when we arrive to Reno. I'm not sure what our reception will be, so I need you prepared for anything."

"I will be," she said as she stood from the table. "Thank you for the coffee."

Jimmy stood, dropped some change on the table and placed his hand on her lower back to guide her back to their sleeper car. He motioned for her to go ahead and spoke quietly with Canneo and Danaá a moment before they stepped away from the car and into one next to them. Jimmy must want them rested and prepared, too.

Jimmy entered the car and sat down in the space next to Hope. She turned and brushed her chin against his shoulder, delighting in his masculine scent, and gazed at him.

Jimmy pressed his lips gently to her forehead, his hand trembling as he brought it to cup her jaw.

"Get some rest, love."

Hope suddenly felt her limbs grow heavy and her eyelids refused to part. She curled up in the seat next to him and was asleep in an instant. Her dreams took on a greenish hue. There was a man with a hat pulled low over his face with a toothy grin that made her shudder. He wanted something.

15

The train pulled into the Reno station in the bright morning sun. Jimmy was on high alert, and thanks to the amorous couple in the car next to them, he felt powerful, strong enough to take on his brothers and whatever army they presented him with. He woke his family, and the women quietly readied the babies and themselves for their greeting party.

And what a party it was. He was grateful Joaquin had given him Canneo and Danaá. The two young men were powerful *brujas*, and as members of the Del Oro family, they were valuable assets. Jimmy knew Joaquin had entrusted them to him for their protection, as well. They were warriors, but they were also young men who needed guidance. He would not let them be seduced by the unholy power in this place.

Canneo and Danaá carried the bags for the women, who carried the babies. Jimmy paid a porter to collect the rest of their things and they descended the train onto the platform. Joaquin had ordered two cars for them, but he'd opted not to contact his brothers. He had a feeling they'd know he was coming anyway. That thought was confirmed moments later as he heard his name called.

"Mr. Manwaring."

Jimmy turned to see a familiar face. Familiar, but wrong, somehow.

Rufus Monroe approached him with a smile flanked by his lovely wife Katherine and two men Jimmy didn't recognize. He stuck out his hand and Jimmy took it, speechless.

"Rufus Monroe. So nice to see you again," he said with a knowing look. "You remember my wife?"

Jimmy shook her hand and she gave him a warm smile. "Good to see you, Mr. Manwaring."

"Katherine and I have been so looking forward to seeing you again. And who do we have here?"

"I'd like to introduce you to my...wife, Hope Manwaring, and our dear companion, Miss Bonnie Collins. She is godmother to our children. And Canneo and Danaá Del Oro are my associates."

Rufus's eyes flared as he sensed the mistruths Jimmy spoke, but Jimmy intended only for his brothers to know the truth about his family.

Katherine peered over the bundles the women were carrying. "And who are these precious ones?"

Hope glanced at Jimmy and smiled. "Byron...and Bonnie. They're only three weeks old and a bit tired out from our travels."

Jimmy saw the tear that rolled from Bonnie's eye as she smiled at the Monroes. She quickly dabbed at it with a handkerchief she had in the pocket of her skirts.

"Well, then," Rufus said, clapping his hands together. "We must get you settled in. We've prepared rooms at our inn, under the orders of your brother. He and William are anxious to see you...all."

Jimmy cleared his throat and nodded to his family. "That will be splendid. The town has changed so much. I am anxious to see what you all have been up to."

The fact that his words were loaded did not go unnoticed by Rufus, but Katherine seemed to be smitten with the babies as she chatted happily with Bonnie and Hope, both of whom kept an eye on Jimmy for a clue as to how they should act.

"Very well. I have instructed your drivers to take you and your things to the hotel. You may rest up there, and then tonight we will dine at Lionel's compound."

Compound. Jimmy didn't like the sound of that. "I appreciate the hospitality, but our travels here were hard on my family. It would be much better if my brothers came to meet us."

Rufus stared him down for several long moments. Jimmy wasn't sure what his position was with his brothers' business any longer, but the fact that he was standing here looking younger and healthier than ever led Jimmy to assume that Rufus and Katherine were not only under Lionel's influence, but that they had their own share of the silver. The fact that they still ran an inn after all this time supported this theory. They'd need the energy to feed them as well.

"Very well, Jimmy. I'm sure your family needs their rest. We shall go to the inn, and I'll let your brothers know there's been a change in plans."

Jimmy's heart skipped a bit. He had to know. "William and... Nathaniel...Will they be joining us as well?"

Rufus gave him a sad smile. "William will be present. As for Nathaniel, we're not quite sure of his location at the moment."

But he was alive. That was all Jimmy needed to hear. A part of him was counting on Nathaniel still having a piece of his humanity, that he might still be someone Jimmy could count on.

The party moved together through the train depot toward the street where two luxurious cars were parked. The two men with Rufus aided Canneo and Danaá in placing their belongings in the first car, and the four of them climbed into the second car. Jimmy and his women and the babies rode in the car with Rufus at the wheel and Katherine at his side.

Rufus spoke generally about the growth of Reno over the past decade, being careful not to mention just how long it had been since Jonah Bane ran off with his daughter Julianna, and Jimmy appreciated that fact. His women were unaware of the connection, and he wanted to be able to tell them in private before they were assaulted with that bit of reality. These were his in-laws, the people he'd stolen a daughter from in the dark of night, the family that lost so much to his brothers, and yet they seemed so...happy. Perhaps Lionel's influence had helped them forget their pain. That would be the only good use of it, to be honest.

The cars pulled up to the front of the Reno Inn, and Jimmy was shocked at the grandiosity of the place.

"Our business continues to cater to the dignitaries of Nevada, celebrities, and even the wealthy seeking a quick marriage or divorce. Our inn offers all of the luxury money can buy that is available this side of the Mississippi, including the first electric elevator, indoor plumbing for the entire hotel including private baths for each of the rooms, and temperature control. We've had a full house for most of the past several years," Rufus said, turning to look at Jimmy seriously, "but there's always room for family."

Jimmy nodded and reached for his hand. "And I am grateful you are so generous to host my family."

Rufus nodded and kept eye contact with Jimmy for several moments, unspoken feelings of regret passing between them.

A doorman let them in to an elaborately decorated hall complete with marble and chandeliers...made of silver. In fact, there were touches of silver everywhere, enough to make Jimmy's stomach turn.

"We had the marble imported, and the silver came mostly from the Comstock Lode, which is what brought our family a healthy business for generations," Katherine was telling Hope and Bonnie.

Jimmy could only hope it was true. But he couldn't ignore the pull. There was cursed silver here. And a lot of it. It called to him, just as it did seventy years ago. He was almost bowled over by the effect. His knees shook and he felt his veins pulsing. He sucked in a breath to try to get it under control before everyone saw the marks on his skin.

Bonnie nudged him. "Jimmy, would you mind taking the babe? I'm afraid my arm is getting tired."

She looked at him knowingly, perhaps assuming holding the baby would help to center him, and she was right. One look into his son's feisty eyes, and he was drawn in by the little man's energy. His heart slowed to a normal rate and he smiled.

"They've got to be hungry," Jimmy said to Hope, really looking at her for the first time since they stepped off the train.

She smiled, but it was obvious she was weary. Jimmy put his spare arm around her and pulled her close. "Just a few more minutes, love, and you all can rest." He looked to Bonnie, but instead of exhaustion, she seemed invigorated, her eyes wide as saucers as she glanced around the lobby of the swanky hotel.

Katherine approached the desk first and received three room keys, which she brought to them. "Here are your rooms. They are part of a suite on the top floor. Ned will show you upstairs and help you get settled."

A bellman sidled up to the group with a smile and an eagerness that nearly made Jimmy chuckle.

"If you'll just follow me, Mr. and Mrs. Manwaring and guests."

He led them to an elevator and two more men carried their things up the four flights of stairs. Hope and Bonnie gawked at the first electric elevator they'd ever seen. Jimmy was too tense to be looking around at all of the extravagance the Monroes had put into their place. He wanted to be happy for them, but he knew why they were so successful and it wasn't just from hard work. They would be over one hundred years old by now, an unheard-of age for most folks, and yet they hadn't changed since Jonah Bane left. Correction, they hadn't changed for the *worse* since then. They had gotten better with age, and that gift was from the silver. Jimmy experienced it too.

On the short lift in the elevator and the quick walk to their suite of rooms, the bellman chatted amiably with Jimmy's ladies about the babies and shared with them the places nearby they could shop for supplies for themselves as well as the children. Jimmy might be able to send them off shopping with Canneo and Danaá eventually, but not having them and the babies right under his nose terrified him.

"I hope you will find your rooms to your liking." The bellman led them into a luxurious suite with a large sitting room, more marble counters, heavily detailed black and silver wallpaper, silver candelabra on a glorious black grand piano, which had Jimmy wondering how the hell they got it up to the top floor, a large bank of windows covered with heavy gray velvet drapes, and more crystal in the chandelier than Jimmy had ever seen in one place. They certainly spared no expense in crafting this extravagance.

"Mr. and Mrs. Manwaring, your room is through here. Your companions have separate rooms on the right-hand side of the suite. Mr. Monroe also ordered a pair of bassinets be arranged for your children."

Jimmy's head was still swimming, and he knew he needed to keep it together. Hope's laughter woke Jimmy from his worries.

Bonnie took Byron from Jimmy's arms, and she and Hope whisked the children away to the bedroom, glancing back over their shoulders toward him with wide eyes. The bellman stood there smiling at him as though waiting for Jimmy to answer a question he hadn't heard.

"This will be fine, thank you."

He reached in his coat pocket and brought out a hefty tip. The bellman's eyes flared in surprise, and he bowed graciously as he left the room, letting them know he was available for anything they might need. He left the room whispering giddily to himself.

Jimmy exhaled and looked around the room. Just how much money had his brothers made in the years since he left?

"Jimmy?"

He hurried into the bedroom at the alarm in Bonnie's voice.

"What's wrong?"

"Nothing," Hope said. She sat with slumped shoulders on the side of the bed. "Nothing, I'm just tired."

"She needs food and rest, Jimmy. Can you—"

"Of course! Let me just run downstairs. Canneo and Danaá are right across the sitting area in their room, alright? Don't answer the door for anyone, do you hear me?"

Bonnie's eyes flared at the command in his voice, but she nodded. Jimmy was hoping she would continue to accept that she needed to do as he said if they were to stay safe.

Jimmy ran downstairs in a hurry but composed himself before approaching the front desk.

"What can I do for you, Mr. Manwaring?"

The young woman at the front desk smiled appreciatively at him. He had no idea whether anyone else knew who he was other than the Monroes, so trust would be an issue with anyone he came across.

"I was hoping it would be possible for someone to bring some food up for my family and guests. We've been traveling a long time and my wife is exhausted. When she's tired, the babies don't get fed, you know what I mean?"

He poured on the charm and sure enough, the young women's eyes sparkled with her desire to serve. He imagined she was probably under some sort of influence, or just so good at her job that she didn't ask too many questions about the clientele staying at the hotel.

"Yes, Mr. Manwaring. We have an excellent chef who would be delighted to prepare you all a feast. I'll make sure it's brought right up."

"Thank you," he looked at her name tag, "Martha. I appreciate your personal attention to this matter. I'll show my gratitude when you arrive."

She blushed and looked away as a coy young lady would do, but it seemed practiced. She'd have to be very good at her job to last long working in league with his brothers and the Monroes. Jimmy wasn't quite sure how involved his brothers were in the business at the inn, but he knew there was tainted silver here. That was enough to have him wary of anyone employed in this endeavor.

"Oh, Mr. Manwaring?"

Katherine hurried over to where Jimmy was preparing to climb the stairs.

"Yes, Mrs. Monroe?"

Katherine looked around to detect any listeners before speaking. "We've rearranged tonight's dinner to be held here at the hotel, so you and your women don't have to travel any more than necessary. Your brothers will be here at seven this evening. Please let me know if you and your guests will be needing formal attire."

"We will," he replied, "I'm afraid we had to leave in a rush and were not able to bring all of our belongings. We'll be needing plenty."

"I can imagine. Especially with the children."

Her voice caught and Jimmy felt a deep pang of regret.

"Katherine..."

"I understand, Jonah. I do not blame you and Julianna for leaving. If we would have known..." She exhaled and her bottom lip quivered. "Well, none of us knew. We did the best we could with what we were given—"

"I am truly sorry for—"

"Don't be," she said, her demeanor changing to that of business-woman. "It was a long time ago. Rufus and I have had a good life. Perhaps it wasn't what we dreamed of when we came to Nevada Territory, but we have found happiness despite losing our daughters."

Jimmy blanched at that. All three? Elizabeth had been married to Lionel, and Victoria...

Jimmy wished yet again that he and his brothers would have lived out their lives in Utah Territory and never set foot in Lake's Crossing all those years ago.

"Thank you. Young Martha at the front desk was very helpful. She's bringing us food."

"That's wonderful. Thank you for letting me know. She does very well in her job. She can handle just about anything that walks through that door."

Jimmy smiled. "She'd have to working in this town."

Katherine shot him a knowing look. "We'll be seeing you at seven. Martha will send for the items you'll need."

"Thank you, Katherine. I appreciate all you've done for my family."

She smiled and touched his arm. "You've done well for yourself, Jonah. I'm glad to see you."

She turned and left before he could say anything else.

Jimmy took a moment to collect himself before climbing the stairs again to the fourth floor. He used his key to open the suite and heard the babies crying instantly. He rushed to the door and found two very frightened women, and two terrified children.

"What—"

"Jimmy! Thank God you came back when you did. She was—"

"It was horrible!"

Both Hope and Bonnie clutched the crying babies to their chest and huddled against him. Their skin was cold to the touch.

"What happened?"

The women looked at each other and then at Jimmy, but they were so frightened they couldn't put words together. He ushered them out into the sitting area so he could call for the men and they sat close to each other, trying to calm the shrieking children.

At his call, Danaá came running out of their bedroom, his clothes torn to shreds. "I cannot wake Canneo."

"Stay with the women," Jimmy ordered, and he rushed into the room.

Canneo lay prone on the bed, his arms flung out to the sides. He was motionless, so much so that Jimmy could barely tell if he was breathing. He shook the young man and then placed a hand on his chest to see if his heart was beating. With his influence, Jimmy sent tendrils of power into the man's body, massaging the organ that kept his lifeforce flowing until it began to pump rapidly, and Canneo sucked in desperately needed oxygen.

"There is danger here," he finally spoke before a coughing fit interrupted him. Jimmy helped him sit up and tried to be patient as the young man caught his breath.

"What did you see?"

Canneo blinked and stared ahead. "A woman. It was horrible. Her face was a mask of anger, she exuded vengeance." Canneo looked to Jimmy, his eyes wide. "She knows you, she...Before I could do anything, before I could act to protect the women, she took my breath from me, pulled it right from my chest."

Jimmy stood quickly and moved to the doorway. Danaá stood at attention, using his body to protect the women as he scanned the room for any signs the intruder returned.

"Where did she go?"

Danaá spoke. "She vanished. When you came through the door."

He closed his eyes and turned, inhaling deeply. "Her energy is no longer present."

"You could smell her?"

"I smelled her, too. She smelled, well, kind of metallic. Like...ore."

Ore. *The silver.* Perhaps her exposure to it in life had left a mark that followed her into the afterlife?

"We'll have to be on alert. If she returns..." Jimmy would find out what she wanted with his family.

A knock on the door startled everyone, and the babies started to cry once more.

"It's food from the restaurant."

He took the few brief moments he had before reaching the door to smooth back his hair and put a pleasant expression on his face when in reality, he felt his control slipping away.

He glanced out the peephole and saw the bellman they'd met previously along with a server from the kitchen pushing a large food cart with covered dishes, the finest utensils and glassware, a pot of tea with cups and saucers made of fine china. He opened the door and breathed in deeply, hoping he would detect nothing but savory foods out in the hall.

"Mr. Manwaring, Chef Robicheaux sends up his regards and this meal he hopes is to your liking."

"Thank you, Ned. I appreciate it." He tipped him generously. "Send my thank you to the chef and his staff."

Jimmy wheeled the cart into the sitting area and began placing the trays on the coffee table in front of his women. He took the babies from them and walked around the room, willing them to relax. It took more effort than usual as they were quite wound up.

"Aren't you going to eat?" Hope asked him, her face still drawn from the travel and then the fright she suffered.

"You all eat first. Then rest. I have a feeling today's not quite through with us."

She frowned. "What is it?"

Jimmy sighed. "There are so many foes. I feel like I'm going in blind. I have no one I trust here to let me know what is going on. I've kept tabs on them as much as possible, but there's not a lot of information traveling freely through the wire or in the newspapers. Joaquin was a good source, but even he doesn't know exactly what's going on here." He swallowed hard. "I had no idea about the ghost."

"How could you have known? She didn't hurt us," Hope said in a low voice. "But I believe she wanted to. I hope she doesn't come back."

Jimmy frowned. "She will never hurt you or the children."

And he would make sure of that. He needed to talk to the young men and see what they knew about warding a home against this kind of invasion.

THAT AFTERNOON the women and the babies slept while he and Canneo and Danaá devised a plan. Two of them would always be with the women and babies. They would sleep in shifts. Jimmy was tempted to seek more help, to perhaps call for Miranda to be with the children, but he'd see what happened when he met with his brothers. Then he'd know what they were up against. If they had to flee…Well, he'd be prepared for whatever was necessary to protect his family.

Katherine herself came up in the early evening with several packages.

"I wasn't sure if your ladies had formal wear for our gathering this evening, and Martha wanted to be sure the dining room was set to her standards, so I took the liberty…"

"Thank you, Mrs. Monroe," Bonnie said as she took the bags. "Jimmy, Hope, and I will just go change."

Bonnie led a giggling Hope into the bedroom and shut the door.

"Thank you, Katherine."

She nodded. "There are suits for the three of you as well." She smiled and turned to leave. At the door she paused. "Your brothers will be here at seven. We'll see you downstairs."

She closed the door and Jimmy turned to the men.

"Remember, do not touch the silverware until I've given you the signal. Do not eat or drink anything until I've been able to check it for contamination. My brothers and I are able to manipulate the chemistry of matter—"

"Tío Joaquin taught us to tell the difference. It is something he can do as well," Canneo said.

Jimmy sighed with relief. They hadn't had the time to debrief what all they knew about the brothers Bane and their terrible gift. "I'm glad your uncle has prepared you. But there is only so much preparation you can have. Even I don't know their current strength. It's been...a very long time."

Danaá stood before Jimmy and exhaled. He reached out and grasped Jimmy by the shoulder, and then placed his other hand on Jimmy's temple.

A brilliant blast of light flared behind Jimmy's closed eyelids, and he tensed as Danaá gave him a taste of his strong medicine...his power. He and Canneo were very powerful indeed. Joaquin had done him an enormous favor granting him these two guardians. Though they had more to learn at Jimmy's side, they would be his brothers in battle.

The creak of a door brought Jimmy's attention to the bedroom from which Bonnie and Hope emerged in gorgeous evening wear. Bonnie wore a light green color that brought out her eyes. The satin draped seductively over her breasts and down her shapely hips. The fabric clung to her shoulders and she wore a long strand of pearls. Jimmy had never seen her look quite so lovely.

But Hope completely took his breath away. Her dress was of a similar cut but in a silver satin. He didn't think it was possible for her to look more naked than she did with no clothes on. Her hair was pulled back with a comb and her expression was unsure. Bonnie fussed at her for a moment, handing her a shawl to drape over her shoulders.

Jimmy approached his women, brushing a kiss against Bonnie's cheek. He told her how beautiful she looked before turning his attentions to Hope. He took one of her gloved hands in his and kissed it for a long moment, his eyes never leaving hers.

Hope came alive under his gaze and the final traces of her uncertainty and exhaustion faded away. She smiled shyly, but Jimmy understood in that moment that she truly wanted him. It went beyond gratitude for saving her and her lover and children. The woman in her wanted the man he was, and damn if Jimmy didn't want to forget about his brothers and the hell poised to rain down upon them and just lose himself in the touch of his woman.

"Jimmy? What do you think?"

Bonnie nudged him and Jimmy realized she'd been talking to him, probably for some time. He smiled at her apologetically and she rolled her eyes.

"I know, I know. You two would just eat each other up if we didn't have other things to attend to. What I was asking is how do you want to handle the babies?"

"I think I should wire Joaquin and ask him to send Miranda to help us. There's just not enough of us to protect them. I'd prefer them be nowhere near my brothers, but I don't want to leave anyone behind—"

"My brother and I will stay here with them, if you like Mr. Manwaring," Canneo said. "That might be best. They are a vulnerability you do not need to worry on tonight."

He was right. "But what if—"

Jimmy felt a sharp pain in his temple and then felt Danaá's presence under his skin. He spun around to look at the younger man, a shudder working its way through his body.

"My brother can...drift, I guess is the right word. If there is trouble, he will alert you. We have warded this room to keep out any visitors like we had earlier."

Jimmy nodded and sucked in a breath. He heard Hope telling the brothers that the babies had just been fed and should be okay for the next two hours, but he needed to see them. He entered the room and his eyes stung with tears as he approached their bassinet. Katherine had arranged such a lovely place for his babies to sleep. The crib was wrapped in gauze and ribbons of pink and blue. She'd even brought a lovely quilt that had flowers and butterflies embroidered on it. He closed his eyes and reached out with the darkness inside him to sense whether there was any hidden silver near the children. Nothing.

Jimmy leaned close, inhaling the babies' scent that calmed his inner beast more than any other elixir on earth. They looked so calm in sleep, curled together likely as they were in the womb. She with her chubby, serene sort of half-smile, and he with his frown and bottom lip that poked out in a perpetual pout. Their personalities were so different, already at just three weeks old, and already he was so in love with them he could not imagine a life without them, and therefore was loath to leave them. He wished his brothers would have given them a couple of days to settle in.

Better to get this confrontation over with before he determined whether or not they could settle here.

He rejoined his women and the brothers in the sitting area.

"You'll...alert me? If there is anything of concern?"

Canneo and Danaá bowed to his request.

He turned to his ladies and held out his arms. "Well, then, the missus Manwaring, let us meet our adversaries and determine what is to be our fate here in Reno."

Each of the women slid their hand into the crook of his arm and smiled up at him. If this were any other circumstance he would almost feel boastful at having such stunning ladies on his arm. But these circumstances had him unsettled and justifiably angry. He shouldn't have to fear bringing his chosen family to meet the family he was born to, and yet here they were.

16

ope wanted to delight in being able to walk into a room on the arm of a handsome man, dressed in finery and looking like a million bucks, but the tension rolling off Jimmy made her stiff with fear. He'd shared some of his past. She knew his brothers had involved themselves with some things he couldn't be a part of and keep a clean conscience. But just how bad were they talking? Like financial, cheating on their taxes? Hurting people, or even murder?

"Boy, your mother-in-law has some style, Jimmy. These dresses and underthings are fabulous."

His lip twitched, but no smile. Hope could tell Bonnie was trying to distract him, but he was under a lot of pressure.

"Yes, please thank her for us," Hope whispered as they neared the doors to the restaurant.

Jimmy paused and inhaled. A frown creased his brow and he cleared his throat. "I want you two to be ready to leave if I tell you to. Canneo and Danaá will protect the babies. Get to them if things go wrong—"

"Jimmy, honey. Relax. Your brothers aren't going to attack. They need you for something as well," Bonnie said.

Jimmy turned to look at her sharply. "What do you mean?"

Bonnie shrugged and gave him a dazzling smile. "I can just tell. That and when Katherine was here, I touched her arm. It has something to do with—"

The doors flew open in front of them. A long table was set with so much crystal and silver, the glare from the fancy chandeliers nearly blinded Hope. She tried to put on a brave smile, but her knees were knocking.

Jimmy led them forward into the room and the doors closed behind them. Hope turned to see two young men in formal serving wear standing there waiting for instructions.

"Praise be. Our brother has returned to us. Come here and let me look at you."

A man not much older than Jimmy stood from the head of the table with his hands out, waiting eagerly to embrace him. He wore a plain black suit, white shirt and black tie, but there was nothing plain about him. He exuded power, much like Jimmy, but his power did not hold the purity or the goodness that Hope felt when she was with her soon-to-be-husband.

Jimmy paused but led them forward.

"Lionel," he said, reaching out a hand to shake.

Lionel glanced at the hand briefly before bringing Jimmy in for a brotherly hug with lots of pounding on Jimmy's back. Then Lionel grabbed him by the face and kissed him hard on the lips, taking Jimmy by surprise. Lionel pressed their foreheads together and said in a low voice, "It's good to have you back."

Jimmy exhaled, as though this reception let him breathe a little easier.

"It's good to see you, brother."

Hope heard a catch in his voice as he answered his brother. His expression was vulnerable for the split second it took for him to step back and collect himself, and then it returned to his usual serious countenance.

"And this is my wife, Gladys."

A very young woman, not much older than eighteen years, stepped forward with a gloved hand out to Jimmy.

"How do you do?" she asked in a thick southern accent. She looked just like the quintessential flapper—thin, with the exception of a small but noticeable baby bump.

Jimmy took her hand like a gentleman, but Hope saw him wince when he noticed her condition.

"Lionel, Gladys, this is my fiancée Hope Johnson, and our companion Bonnie Collins."

Lionel's eyes flared as he gave Hope a onceover. Goosebumps rose on her exposed skin, and she felt ill the moment he touched her.

"You are indeed a beauty," Lionel said, bending to kiss the back of her hand. "And Miss Collins, so lovely to meet you as well." He lingered over Bonnie's hand for a moment and she chuckled. "I hope your travels were comfortable?"

"Yes they were, thank you," Hope said, her throat dry. She swallowed to try to alleviate the discomfort. Music played from a Victrola in the corner of the room, and servers came and went, carrying bottles of wine to the table. Jimmy watched it all, a scowl forming on his face.

"Let us take our seats. Dinner will be served momentarily. Please, Hope, sit here," Lionel said, gesturing to his left side and pulling out the chair for her. Gladys was seated at his right by one of the servers, an enthusiastic smile on her face.

"Rufus and Katherine won't be joining us?" Bonnie asked.

"I'm afraid they have hotel business to attend to this evening," Lionel answered, giving Bonnie a curious appraisal. Hope wondered if Bonnie felt as uncomfortable as she did under the man's scrutiny.

"Where is William?" Jimmy asked Lionel as he held out the chair next to Hope for Bonnie, and then took the seat next to her. Hope watched him curiously, wondering why he didn't sit at the other head of the table. He watched his brother intently, keeping his long arm across the back of Bonnie's chair, his hand resting so that his fingers gently brushed Hope's shoulder. His touch soothed her and some of her unease drifted away.

"He's out of town, actually. He went to Denver on personal business. He should return in a day or so."

Jimmy looked grim when he nodded. Perhaps it was good, Hope thought, that they only had one brother to contend with.

Soft murmurings of thanks were given as the servers came forward with dinner salads for everyone. They poured the wine, which Hope ignored, reaching for her water instead.

"I'd like to propose a toast and then say grace," Lionel said, standing from his seat. Everyone watched as his eyes glanced over at his guests and landed squarely on his brother.

"It is with great joy I welcome my youngest brother home to the place we were called to by our Lord. It is my hope that we can mend the rifts of our past and move forward in strength and harmony as we continue to build the civilization as we were sent here to do so long ago. I welcome my brother's lovely companions. I am delighted to see him happy after so long." He raised his glass and the diners all toasted. Gladys watched him with love in her eyes, and Hope wondered if he truly was a monster or if somewhere deep down there was something redeemable about the man.

"Thank you, brother." Jimmy said, taking a sip of his wine. He let it rest upon his tongue for a moment before swallowing it down. He'd warned Hope and Bonnie that his brother might attempt to manipulate their food and drink to make them more receptive to him. He'd urged them not to drink wine, and he'd also told them that he would alert them if they were not to touch the utensils laid out for them. Hope had the excuse of the babies, but Bonnie partook of the wine. She seemed unaffected after her first drink, but Hope would continue to watch her.

"Now, if we may all join hands," he said as he took Hope's hand in his. Hope looked to Jimmy. His nostrils flared but he showed no other displeasure. Hope disliked the feel of Lionel's hand in hers. It was cold and dry as though he'd been outside too long on a Midwest winter day. He let his thumb drift over the back of her hand and she felt a desperate urge to pull it away, but she held steady so as not to disturb the moment.

"Our heavenly Father," Lionel began, his head lowered in prayer. "We thank you for the gifts you have given us, for thy sustenance you've provided for us and our families. We're grateful our brother has come home to resume his part of our glorious mission and that he's brought these beautiful women to join our community. In your name we pray, dear Lord, and ask that you bless us and deliver us from evil. Amen."

Hushed amens were spoken around the table. Hope watched as Jimmy took a long drink of his wine, nearly draining the glass. A server stepped forward and filled it the moment he set it down.

They ate their salads making small talk here and there. Hope learned Gladys was from South Carolina and had come to Nevada to study at the university here, but upon meeting Lionel, she abandoned her studies and joined his religious organization. They were married six months ago and they were expecting their first child in about five months. Hope and Gladys talked about the joys and pains of pregnancy, with Bonnie sharing some of their adventures. Jimmy remained silent, caught in some sort of a staring duel with Lionel.

"Well, I'm awfully glad you'll be here when my time comes. It will be nice to have someone here who's been through it before."

"Yes," Lionel said, his eerie gaze falling on Hope. "We are so glad you and your children are here. We've been without children for so long."

Hope rested her hands in her lap to hide how shaky they were. She was terrified of this man.

Jimmy brushed his fingers on her shoulder once more to reassure her before he spoke.

"Yes, I've wondered about how your *family* has fared all these years."

Gladys dropped her fork onto her plate and the clanging sound startled Hope.

For a brief moment, Lionel's face twisted into a mask of pain and sorrow before returning to an almost indignant expression.

"These are matters for us to discuss after we've dined, brother."

Jimmy raised an eyebrow at him and drank more wine.

The rest of the meal passed with little discussion. When the servers had cleared most of the dishes, Lionel leaned back in his chair.

"Ladies, I'm not sure if your companion has shared with you much of our early lives together, but it has always been a tradition in our family that we enjoy music. Brother, sing for the ladies."

Jimmy's cheeks flushed and he looked to Bonnie and Hope. Hope watched as he looked around the room and knew the moment his eyes landed on the upright piano in the corner of the dining room.

"I'll play for you, but I don't sing anymore."

Jimmy stood and strolled over to the piano, his back to the group. Hope slid closer to Bonnie in her chair and Bonnie reached for her hand under the table. Hope tried to discern how Bonnie was feeling about this evening. She didn't seem nearly as unnerved as Hope felt, more like she was fascinated with the developments.

Jimmy stretched out his long arms and began to play a familiar tune that Hope recognized from his time playing at the saloon. It was one of his favorites, she thought, because it was one of the ones he'd play nearly every night. She'd missed hearing him play. She stood from her chair and went to stand next to the piano.

Jimmy's hands flew over the keys and the tension in his shoulders bled out. One song turned into two, then three...Bonnie came over and put her arm around Hope's waist, squeezing her just enough to help calm her nerves.

"Just hang in there a little longer, honey," Bonnie whispered to her. "Jimmy knows what he's doing."

Hope sighed and leaned into her. The combination of Jimmy's music and Bonnie's touch soothed her to the point she almost forgot they needed to be on alert. Until Lionel suddenly appeared at her back and placed his cold hand on her shoulder.

"That sounds wonderful, brother. You've really improved your musicianship over the years, haven't you?"

Jimmy shrugged. "Playing in saloons nightly will do that." He turned to face Lionel with a frown. "I'd like to take my ladies up to the room to rest. Then I would like to come down here and discuss some things with you."

It didn't sound like a request, more like the confrontation would not take place in front of Hope and Bonnie.

"Oh, but won't you ladies please stay for dessert?"

Sure enough, the kitchen staff brought out plates to each of the guests with a single slice of decadent, several-layered chocolate cake. Hope had never seen cake like this in person, only in the movies she used to sneak off to see in the years before she was married, back when the picture shows were new. There were chocolate swirls on the plate, a garnish of fruit, and the servers poured small glasses of a dessert wine. Hope and Bonnie looked at each other and giggled before returning to their seats.

Jimmy didn't follow right away. He was still locked in some form of nonverbal conversation with Lionel that frightened Hope the more she thought about it. What could be so terrible? What happened between these two for Jimmy to hold such a multitude of emotions for his brother? She'd seen every expression pass across his face from anger, disgust, regret, sorrow, and even loneliness. She had to imagine he'd been lonely for a long time before joining her and Bonnie.

Jimmy leaned down between them and whispered, "I don't feel right about this. There's something..."

Bonnie lifted a fork full of the chocolate cake to her lips and paused. She closed her eyes and shuddered before lowering her fork to the table.

"I think I need to lie down," she finally said. She opened her eyes and leveled a glare at Lionel. "It's been a really long day. Please forgive us, but Hope and I need to tend to the babies and rest."

She pushed back her chair and stood, wobbling a little before Jimmy steadied her. He placed a hand at the small of her back and Hope walked on her other side, taking her weight. Bonnie seemed very woozy, which made Hope very happy she hadn't tried the cake.

"I'll just see them to the room and I'll be back to speak to you, Lionel."

Hope glanced back to see Lionel delicately taking a bite of chocolate cake from the fork his wife was holding.

"Mmmm, delicious. We'll see you soon," he said, grinning in a devilish way that made Hope's hair stand on end. She couldn't get out of that room fast enough.

17

Jimmy cursed to himself as Bonnie swayed dangerously. They climbed the steps back to their room as quickly as they could with her being in a state similar to being drugged. Jimmy finally scooped her up in his arms and carried her the remaining three flights of stairs.

"Jimmy, what's happening?"

"Let's get her to bed first."

Hope pounded on the door once they returned to the suite. Canneo opened the door and Jimmy swiftly carried Bonnie inside, without straining one bit, over to the bed and lay her down gently.

"What was wrong with the cake, Jimmy?"

Jimmy rested his hands on his hips as he looked down at Bonnie's flushed face. He exhaled and shook his head. How could he have been so naïve?

"It was the silver. I'd checked before we ate dinner and foolishly believed my brother would behave himself. When the wait staff brought the dessert out, I was still at the piano, and though I felt it…"

"What do you mean, you felt it?" Hope asked him, her fear evident in her voice.

Jimmy took Hope's hands in his and led her over to the chaise, glancing at the sleeping babes to ensure they didn't need tending to.

"Hope, you know I'm not like other men, and I've told you some about my past."

"Yes, Jimmy, but I don't understand. What happened? Why did you leave your brothers?"

It was time to tell his betrothed the truth and pray for the best.

"My brothers and I were led here under false pretenses. My brother...Lionel...he believed God brought us here. We were to find an abandoned mine and continue digging until we found a cache of silver. This silver was meant to give us the capital we needed to begin a new civilization here. And all of that came true. We came where Lionel said we would find it. We repaired the mine where it had collapsed, and after several months, we found the silver. But when we touched it—"

"It changed you."

Jimmy's skin was tight, stretched thin over his bones. Just talking about that fateful day when they laid hands upon the ore and felt its power made him crave it deep down in his cellular level. His body thrummed with need he'd been able to keep at bay for so long, but tonight he'd felt his control slipping.

"It changed me forever," Jimmy said, shuddering when he heard the otherworldly sound emanating from his body. "Do not be afraid, Hope. I would never hurt you or the babies—"

"Tell me more. I see how difficult this is for you," she said, sliding her hands into his grip. Her touch anchored him and enabled him to continue speaking.

"We were below ground for a very long time as our bodies were altered by the force behind the evil silver. It's not just a metal or something occurring naturally. This place was unholy, wrong. It affected us all a little differently, but some things we have in common: the ability to influence those around us and to alter matter, incredible strength when we are at our peak, and longevity. But all of this comes at a price. We must feed."

Hope blinked at his words. "Feed? What do you—"

"Energy, love. That which is born of carnal knowledge, of the taking of virgin blood, and of acts of pure love. All the things the creature who brought us to the silver cannot absorb for himself."

"Creature? You mean the devil?"

Jimmy frowned. "I do not believe it is the devil, not like the fallen angel we were taught of as children in the church. But it is darkness. It is void of any love or light, and therefore it craves those things. It uses my brothers and I to increase its power. I left here many years ago because I did not want my wife to fall under the control of the creature or my brothers."

Hope pulled away from him and Jimmy felt her movement like a jolt to his heart. He would never force her to stay, but he prayed she wouldn't run.

"Then why did you bring us here?" Her voice was barely a whisper, and Jimmy could see her trembling. He reached for her but she pulled away once more.

"Because I am stronger now. I understand what I need to do to survive and what it takes to maintain my strength. The creature found us in Grass Valley—"

Hope gasped. "And you brought us, my lover and my children, to its front door? How could you?"

"How could I *not*? I want the children to be safe, all of you to be safe. If it found us in Grass Valley, it would find us anywhere. It promised me it would not harm you or the children if we came here. It will not touch you, I swear. We will stay long enough to be married and for the children to be settled, and then if you want to leave, we will leave. But I must appease the creature if we are to find any peace."

"How can you be sure it will not hurt the children?"

Jimmy didn't want to lie to her, and he truly felt he could protect them, but if he wanted her to trust him, he'd have to be completely forthright.

"Hope..."

"He'll do the best he can, but that might not be enough. We're going to have to trust ourselves and each other if we're going to keep our family together."

Hope and Jimmy rushed to Bonnie's side.

"Are you hurt?" Hope asked Bonnie, taking her hand.

"Not at all. It was just...overwhelming. Jonah, am I—?"

"I don't believe your contact was enough to have altered you. We were down in the ground for over a year. The power of the silver took it's time with us. Others my brothers have conscripted into their power have been subdued with gifts of the silver as jewelry, but not altered in the same way."

Bonnie seemed flushed but unharmed. Jimmy breathed a sigh of relief. She was strong. So was Hope. He knew they would be safe, as long as they could trust each other...

"Should I be calling you Jonah, too?" Hope asked.

Jimmy wasn't sure how he felt about that. Taking on the new identity had allowed him some separation emotionally from all that had occurred with his brothers. Becoming Jonah once more...His brothers would call him Jonah, of that he was sure. When they'd changed their names to avoid detection from anyone back home in Utah Territory, they'd kept their first names as a tie to their parents. It had been important to them then. Would they still insist?

"Jimmy is a good man. Jimmy is the man you trust. I want to continue to be that man for you."

Hope placed a hand on his cheek and Jimmy's heart swelled. Could they trust him? Could he do what he'd sworn to do?

The power continued to pulse under his skin and he *needed*...

"I need to...I must..."

Hope leaned forward and pressed her lips to his, tentatively at first and then with a conviction he'd known she possessed but had only vaguely glimpsed before this. Her action ignited a fire that roared inside him, drowning out the vibrations from his nearness to the silver. He clutched her soft body to him and allowed her love to bathe him in the light he so craved from her.

A small moan escaped her throat and Jimmy could hold back his desire no longer. His tongue slid between her lips and he took the kiss as deep as he dared. Her moan was cut off by her gasp and suddenly she was on his lap, her legs wrapped around his hips and Jimmy nearly lost all control. Hope's hands caressed his jaw and his touch grew greedier with every sweep of their tongues against each other's.

Jimmy felt a pressure against his back and broke the kiss long enough to turn his head. Bonnie rose up on her knees behind him, her hands on his shoulders.

"She wants you, Jimmy. Our Hope needs you."

Hope writhed against him, and the heat from her core warmed his growing cock. It took all of his restraint not to take her and make her his wife in the flesh if not before God, but he'd vowed not to do that.

"Soon," he whispered. He looked down to find his skin streaked in black and knew the greenish hue was cast upon them from his eyes. He hated for them to see him like that, but they'd seen it before and hadn't run in fear. Yet. He prayed that would never happen.

"Jimmy," Hope said, her pelvis rising, her core rubbing against him, the friction driving them both insane with lust.

"Bonnie," Jimmy pleaded. "Please." He needed Bonnie to do what he could not in good conscience do for Hope, not yet. She needed to heal, and he needed them wed before he would touch her so intimately.

Bonnie shifted to his side and helped Hope out of her dress. Jimmy would never get enough of the sight of her bare breasts, and despite his attempts to keep his lust at bay, he couldn't help but touch what was so tantalizingly displayed before him. Hope placed his hands firmly on her breasts and threw her head back. Bonnie captured her lips and slid her hand down Hope's stomach and under Hope's panties.

Hope cried out and began to move again, more frantic this time, and the friction of both Hope's core and the back of Bonnie's hand brushing against Jimmy's cock was almost too much.

"Kiss him," Bonnie whispered. "Let me make you feel good."

Hope's expression was one of rapture as Jimmy kissed her deeply.

Her hands rested on his shoulders for balance, but that was the most she could manage as Bonnie's touch brought her closer and closer to ecstasy.

Jimmy's whole body trembled with the energy he consumed from this act between them. He reached for Hope's hips and pulled her even tighter against his and they both moved in concert with Bonnie's hand until all three of them were drenched with sweat. Jimmy's eyes locked on Bonnie's and she smiled excitedly.

"You two are so beautiful together. Let me watch you come, baby. Come for us," she whispered into Hope's ear before swirling her tongue along the sensitive flesh.

Hope cried out in earnest and she froze. Her back arched and her thighs quaked as a forceful orgasm shook her to her core. Jimmy held her, tasting the flesh of her neck as he absorbed all of the love and energy her body released. Bonnie's hand continued to caress her gently, wringing every last drop of satisfaction from Hope's body.

Jimmy watched his women kiss and he felt the need subside. He was so sated by their lovemaking that he felt that elusive peace he'd been desperate for so close he could almost accept it as reality. These two beautiful women had been sent to him at just the right time, and he prayed that they could move forward together, all three of them, against the evil lurking just outside their door. He almost believed it could be so.

Jimmy lay Hope back gently on the bed and Bonnie went with her, caressing her body. "Thank you for letting me be a part of your love. I cannot tell you enough how much both of you mean to me."

Hope smiled as her eyes drifted closed. "I love you Jimmy," she murmured before turning into Bonnie's shoulder. "I love you, baby."

Bonnie winked at Jimmy before turning her attention to Hope. "I love you, too. And you," she said to Jimmy as she pulled the blanket over the two of them. "You are a welcome addition. Watching the two of you together...You sure are a handsome man. I never thought I'd want a man in my bed but watching you with the woman I love is incredible. And watching you with the children...You've definitely changed my mind about the ability of a man to be good."

Jimmy felt his cheeks flush at her words. He never dreamed he'd find happiness with a woman again, let alone two, but he wouldn't give them up for anything. His relationship with each of them was different, but that's what made their threesome strong. With Hope at the center of their love, they could handle whatever his brothers chose to throw at them. He was sure of that. With Hope's peace and Bonnie's strength, they would be strong enough to raise the children and make a life together. That belief kept Jimmy focused. He knew what he needed to do.

He stood from the bed and glanced once more at the children who were still sleeping soundly. He straightened his clothes and took a deep breath.

"Where are you going?" Bonnie asked. She rested her head in her hand as Hope slept soundly against her side.

"My brother is still here. I am going to lay down some ground rules regarding our staying here, and I'm going to discuss our marriage ceremony."

Bonnie nodded. "The sooner you two are married, the sooner you will take what's yours," she said in a teasing voice.

"That's not what's important. I want the children to have a father and I want them to be safe."

"Of course," she said. "And you want Hope to be your wife—"

"I want you both."

Bonnie's eyes flared. "Jimmy—"

"It can be done in the eyes of God. I know I can't legally be wed to you both—"

"I don't want a husband."

Her words were like a slap to the face.

"But Bonnie—"

"Jimmy, I can take care of myself. I don't want no man having a say over my life. I love Hope, and I'm staying with her, and as much as I can't believe it, I care about you, too. But I'll never get married, Jimmy."

"But I want to take care of you. I want to make sure you're protected and safe and..."

"And you will. I know you will. I actually feel better knowing you'll be marrying her because I know there are things you can do for her that I can't."

"But she needs you, too, Bonnie." Jimmy feared Bonnie might just decide to move on once Jimmy and Hope were married.

"I know that. I'm not going anywhere. Relax. Go see that brother of yours and do what you have to. The sooner the better."

Jimmy nodded. The sooner the better. For many reasons.

LIONEL WAS EXACTLY where Jimmy had left him an hour before, but he was alone. The dining room was dark except for candlelight in the middle of the table they'd dined on. He sipped whisky from a crystal glass that sparkled from the candlelight.

"Are you feeling better, brother?"

Jimmy wanted to slap the smirk off of his face, but then he reminded himself he needed his brother's help.

"Don't ask questions you already know the answers to," he said. He felt rather petulant, a feeling he hadn't experienced since he'd left this place.

"My apologies. I know I have a lot to atone for with you. Please. Sit and drink with me. Let us discuss what has brought you back to me."

Jimmy accepted the glass and welcomed the burn as it made its way to his center.

"Your women are exquisite. Tell me, how is it that my straight-laced brother ended up with two beautiful women on his arms?"

Jimmy leaned back in the chair and finished off his whisky. "I'm not sure what forces were at work, but let's just say Julianna warned me this would come to pass. I'd been waiting for hope, and Hope arrived with Bonnie."

"I see. And I'm under the impression that you've come here to be married."

Jimmy rested his elbows on the table. "I would like you to marry us, yes. But I also felt it was time to reconnect with my brothers."

Lionel poured them both more of the amber liquid. Jimmy watched the light play on the glass and reached out with his senses to be sure Lionel wasn't working any of his skill upon the alcohol.

"Reconnect. Yes. Our reunion is long overdue. Things are about to change in this country, and while I fully intend to keep our interests here in Reno protected by any means necessary, I could use your help."

Jimmy frowned. "What do you mean?"

"You'll see it in the papers tomorrow, I suppose. But there's no harm in telling you. The stock markets have crumbled in upon themselves and our economy has taken quite a hit. I imagine many of the wealthiest Americans will be destitute in the coming days, if they aren't already.

Jimmy's pulse quickened. "But that...that's insane! How did it happen?"

Lionel sighed and took a long drag on his whiskey. "Investors have been making risky moves for some time." Lionel leveled a pointed look at Jimmy. "Tell me, brother. Where do you keep your wealth these days?"

Jimmy swallowed, his heart suddenly dry. "I've invested a great deal in the mills and industries in California. I've got my properties and some money put away..."

"Well, I gather then you will not be destroyed by this turn of events, but perhaps not as comfortable as you've been."

God. What if he's right? What if it's gone? Jimmy controlled his breathing and his outward appearance as best as he could to keep his panic from Lionel's notice.

"I'm sure we'll manage. I'll contact my employees in Fort Bragg and let them know to be prepared."

Lionel sipped at his drink and his lips split into a knowing smile. "A good course of action, to be sure."

The calculated way Lionel introduced this topic brought Jimmy's anger simmering to just below the surface. His brother was not going to make this easy.

After a long few moments, Lionel shifted in his chair and laced his fingers in front of him on the table.

"I will marry you and your betrothed. We can do it within the next few days, but I'm going to need something from you in return."

Of course you would, you evil, manipulating son of a—

"Lay out your terms, brother." Jimmy let some of his animosity bleed out in the way he enunciated the word that bound them together. Brothers. Blood.

"I want you to rejoin the family business, either with me at the compound, or if you prefer to tend to the secular side of our business, stay here and run this establishment. Rufus and Katherine have been doing it for a long time and they could use some time off. You and your...family...could live on the premises and oversee the day-to-day operations run smoothly. You'll be surrounded by the *elements* you need to remain strong and you will be close by, which makes all of us stronger, you know."

"Looks to me like you've done just fine on your own," Jimmy said. He raised an eyebrow. "You haven't had me here in over fifty years and yet you've done quite well."

Lionel shrugged and chucked in an attempt to show humility which he did not possess. "William and I have been quite successful persuading others to join our endeavors. Our religious organization is more than a thousand strong, many of whom live outside of town with my family. It is a wonderful place. Oh, you must see it! All of our hard work coming here, finding the mine...I've been able to build just the civilization God wanted me to build and it's a holy place, really beyond my wildest dreams."

"You still want to believe God sent us here." Jimmy couldn't believe his brother was either so blind, so stupid, or so willing to lie to himself and those around him that he would still try to pawn that story off on him.

"Believe what you want, little brother. I have achieved that which I was sent here to do, and I intend to grow my church, spread the word, and with you here, adding to the strength of our family, we can expand even further! During dark times, the people need to feel they are cared for, and I fully intend to be the savior they are looking for!"

"You're insane," Jimmy whispered. "You would drag this evil as far as the eye can see, wouldn't you? You'd take advantage of desperate people to grow your personal empire—"

"My brother, it appears you've forgotten what we learned deep in the earth all those years ago. This is what we were meant to do. For better or worse, Jonah dear. We are tied to this place by blood and the silver, and we may never cease doing its bidding. We have a higher purpose! We—"

"I'll have no part in spreading this evil—"

"You'll do what you must or you risk losing everything you love."

Lionel's voice boomed out across the room, and the faint light surrounding them began to pulse with green. Jimmy felt his anger claw to the surface until he too emanated that eerie green hue from his eyes.

"You'll not threaten me, Lionel. I've sacrificed everything because of you. You will give me what I ask for and you will never harm my family, or God help me—and I mean the God we worshipped before this unholy alliance consumed us—I will end you and this entire civilization. Do not believe for one instant that I am incapable. I have learned much since leaving this place and I have not returned unarmed."

Jimmy had no real idea if his threats were plausible, but there was no way he would ever return to being his brother's lackey. If he and his women and children had to leave this place and live like paupers, he'd do it to protect them, and they would survive. He was strong enough...but the fear the creature would haunt them, would harm his children...That fear is what kept him here making yet another deal with the devil it seemed.

Lionel calmed himself until his voice returned to its normal timbre. A pleasant smile graced his handsome face that had barely changed over the years. If anything, his handsome brother had grown more attractive and had taken on a more youthful appearance over the years.

"Please, Jonah. Let's not quarrel. All I'm asking is that you and your family reside here in Reno, in either the compound or this hotel, and let us attempt to rekindle our familial respect for one another. William may not say it, but he misses you. He's been through terrible ordeals since you left us so abruptly. And Nathaniel—"

"Where is Nathaniel?" Jimmy couldn't help the hopeful tone to his voice. He desperately wished for news of his favorite brother.

Lionel sighed. "Nathaniel is away at the moment, but his...vocation...frequently brings him through this area. He and his...well. He is well, that is all I can tell you, and he is living his truth, just as you have done, but he never leaves for too long before returning with his...mate. I'm sure he will return soon, especially once I send word that our beloved brother has returned."

So he'd dangle that carrot in front of Jimmy to keep him here as well. Jimmy couldn't refuse the chance to reunite with Nathaniel, even if it meant confrontations with William or the machinations of Lionel.

"I have your word my family will not be touched by your influence, your silver, or any evil dealings you've created in this place?"

Lionel nodded slowly, his lips splitting in a triumphant grin. "I wouldn't dream of harming your beautiful family. Please, Jonah... You'll stay? You'll give me the honor of marrying you and your beloved?"

What choice did he have? For all he knew, he was financially ruined, he'd be on the run from the creature, and he'd be putting his children in danger if he left here now. Somehow, he'd have to make this work.

He uttered the words that would seal all of their fate.

"Yes. I'll stay."

18

Two weeks later...

Hope spun around once more in front of the enormous diamond dust mirror and admired the lovely dress Lionel's wife Gladys offered her for the ceremony. They were in Gladys's room in the home she shared with Lionel. It was a massive three-story place with several guest rooms where they would stay tonight after the wedding before returning to their new home in the Inn at Lake's Crossing, newly renamed by Jimmy as he'd taken over the business.

"I wore this dress when we were wed six months ago, and William's wife wore it before me. Those are real crystals sewn into the dress from the local mines."

"It's beautiful," Hope said, her cheeks sore from smiling.

She was really going to marry Jimmy today, after all they'd been through. Her children would have a proper father and she'd have a proper husband. Bonnie would be their companion, and the five of them would live here in this beautiful hotel surrounded by luxury. All they had to do was oversee the hotel's business and share Jimmy with his family from time-to-time. It had turned out much better than she'd hoped.

"You are beautiful," Bonnie said, wrapping her arms around

Hope's waist from the back and pressing a kiss to her cheek. "I can't wait to stand by your side as you marry our Jimmy."

Bonnie had told Hope about her conversation with Jimmy, that she'd refused to become his wife. She understood why, but in her mind's eye she'd conjured up a little fantasy where the three of them were married to each other and spent every night in each other's arms. She wanted that more than anything, wanted Bonnie by her side just as much as Jimmy. But she respected the fact that Bonnie's life before they met had been filled with pain and suffering at the hands of men and therefore never wanted to be beholden to another man again. It would have to be enough, their companionship.

Hope turned in her arms and kissed her on the lips. "I love you," she whispered.

Bonnie's gaze darted toward Gladys before she took the kiss deeper. Gladys knew the nature of their relationship. They'd grown to trust her in the short time they'd been there. She'd shared with them the nature of her situation with Lionel, and they'd been shocked by her candid explanation.

"I'm no fool. I know he is using me for the children I can provide for him. He wants a large family, and he holds me up as an example for the women in the compound. He needs the births, you know, or at least the act of making babies. Jonah explained that to you, I reckon?"

They'd nodded, fully aware of what they'd signed on for when Jimmy became a part of their lives.

"And in exchange, he keeps me in the lifestyle I've grown accustomed to." Gladys held out her hands that were covered in silver jewelry with diamonds and precious stones. She fingered the large silver brooch that held her silk wrap together across her breasts. "I'll never grow old and I'll be beautiful forever with beautiful children in a beautiful place. What more could a girl from Nowhere, South Carolina want?"

It all sounded so simple. Hope just prayed there was nothing more sinister at play here.

"But what about the silver?"

Gladys smiled. "Wearing it makes them stronger. We all benefit from it. What can it hurt?"

Jimmy had insisted Hope and Bonnie not wear it, but if it would be better for him, shouldn't she?

The babies cooed from their bassinet and she walked over to their side. "Oh, you silly babies. I know you've had plenty to eat. Now, mama's got to go marry daddy and then I'll be back to care for you—"

"And then you and Jimmy will be having your wedding night," Bonnie said.

Hope turned to look at her, confused.

"But Bonnie—"

"I will stay with the babies tonight. I want you to have this night, the two of you. It's my gift to you."

"But what if I want you with us?"

Bonnie smiled and smoothed back Hope's curl that had come loose. Bonnie had managed to tame Hope's hair into perfect pincurls that hugged her scalp and looked very fashionable. Hope felt like a goddess in the dress, with the makeup and hairstyle...

"I will be with you in here," she said, placing her hand over Hope's left breast. "But tonight is about you and your husband. Don't worry," she said, letting her fingertip circle Hope's nipple, causing it to pucker against the satin underthings Gladys had brought. "I intend to spend every night going forward worshipping your beautiful body and watching him do the same. I know you'll be in my arms and by my side, and that's all that matters. Jimmy needs to know you feel that way about him, too, and the only way for him to be certain is for you to have this night together, just the two of you."

"Ladies, it's time for the ceremony to begin," Gladys said. She smiled at them both and took each of their hands. "I'm so glad we'll be sisters."

"Thank you for welcoming us into your home, Gladys," Hope said.

"Yes and thank you for making this such a special day for Hope."

Gladys hugged them both and said, "You're both so welcome."

. . .

LIONEL HAD DETERMINED the ceremony should be held in the chapel of the compound, which was in the building adjacent to his home. There were three large apartment buildings on the property as well as a large workshop where the families made jewelry and textiles when they weren't attending classes and worship services with Lionel and William. There were stables for several dozen horses, a barn for livestock, a large communal kitchen for celebrations, and several other buildings that Hope hadn't been told their use. She tried not to be creeped out by the people living here. They were all so nice and welcoming, but there was just something...vacant about them. Jimmy had warned her it was a result of their proximity to the silver. She'd noticed many of them wearing pieces of jewelry made of silver, but it looked normal...until she looked closer. This particular silver had a slightly greenish tint to it. It was still beautiful, and the jewelry she'd seen was lovely, but she now understood why Jimmy always discouraged her to touch it or wear any of it. Gladys had even offered her a delicate silver barrette to wear for something borrowed, but she'd resisted. Gladys assured her that no harm would come from the silver, but Bonnie and Hope had chosen to trust Jimmy in this matter.

The air outside was chilly, which made the short walk to the front of the chapel uncomfortable, but once inside the foyer, it was warm enough that her shivers subsided. Canneo and Danaá followed, each carrying one of the children. Hope was grateful that the young men were with them. They made her feel secure being apart from the children because they'd sworn their lives to protect them. They were loving with the children, often singing to them in their first language which soothed the infants, especially the fussy Byron. Their spiritual and physical strength was apparent in everything they did. Bonnie felt it, too, and she spent a lot of time with them, asking questions about their magic. Hope wasn't sure, but she thought perhaps Bonnie wanted to learn more about herself and thought the men might have answers for her.

The men took the infants inside and Bonnie took Hope's arm. "Are you ready, my love?"

Hope's bouquet of flowers trembled in her hands. "I think so," she said in a shaky voice.

Bonnie turned to face her. "Do you love him?"

"Of course I do," Hope answered.

"And you trust him?"

"With my life and the lives of my children," Hope said with conviction.

Bonnie smiled. "Then go to him. Make your vows with him. Spend the night with him consummating your bond, and then we will be a family."

Hope sniffled a little as tears burned at her eyes. "I love you, Bonnie."

"And I love you, my Hope. Go to him."

The doors to the sanctuary opened, and Hope was greeted by hundreds of unfamiliar faces. She'd known Lionel's congregation would be here, but she wasn't prepared for the shock. All of those expectant smiles, all of those people...

"It's alright," Bonnie whispered. "Just look at him," she exclaimed. "He's so handsome, he takes my breath away."

Hope's eyes blurred from nervous tears but once she spotted Jimmy, everything came into focus.

She'd never seen him look quite so debonair, and that was saying something. She'd watched him wear suits and even tuxedos previously, like the first night they dined at the hotel with Lionel, but this suit he wore for their wedding fit him perfectly. His auburn hair looked almost black slicked back from his face. His green eyes glittered under his serious brows until he saw her.

She watched as he sucked in a breath and his expression changed to one of deep, life-altering, world-changing love.

That was all the encouragement she needed to move forward.

Hushed sounds of appreciation emanated from the congregation as she walked toward the man she loved. When she stood before him, Bonnie gave her arm a squeeze and then lifted Hope's veil over her head.

"You look so lovely," Bonnie said. "Go get our man," she whispered and kissed Hope's cheek.

And then Hope turned to face her betrothed and the rest of the room all fell away.

Hope vaguely recalled hearing Lionel speak the words so commonly expressed during the joining of two people in God's eyes, but all she could think of was how amazing this man before her was and how much she couldn't wait to call him her husband.

When it was time to exchange vows, she was sure she said the right words and he did as well, but what she remembered most was the growing feeling of love filling her up, taking over all of the fear and loss she'd suffered before finding her way to Jimmy.

Bonnie stepped forward with the pillow holding both of their wedding bands and at that moment, Jimmy's expression filled with rage. He turned on Lionel.

"You agreed," he growled, keeping his voice low so as not to alert the entire church there was a problem.

"Jimmy," Hope said. "It's all right. Gladys and I spoke. It's fine. I want to do this for you."

"Brother, you know it is important that the ceremony be done in this way. You must both wear the rings—"

"No. I won't have that touch her skin—"

"Jimmy." Something in her tone caught his attention and his worried gaze fell upon her. She knew he had reason to be leery, but he'd been so very strong for her. It was her turn to be strong for him and to give him this moment. "It's just for tonight."

Jimmy squeezed his eyes shut and exhaled harshly. She felt terrible that he was so conflicted, but she knew this would give him more strength and would hopefully appease his brothers. She and Bonnie had agreed when Gladys approached them with this aspect of the ceremony that it was worth the risk. They knew Jimmy would take care of them, that he would never hurt them or the children, nor would he allow them to be hurt.

Hope held out her hand to Jimmy and waited, hoping he would go through with it.

The several beats she waited were agonizing. She closed her eyes and prayed he would go through with it. And then she felt his hand take hers gently.

"With this ring, I thee wed."

The moment the silver slid onto her finger, she was enveloped in darkness, a black, suffocating blanket of pain that sucked the breath from her lungs and burned like ice.

And then it was gone. She opened her eyes to find Jimmy staring at her in horror, but when she smiled at him, he relaxed.

Hope turned to Bonnie to reach for the ring and she froze. Bonnie's eyes had rolled back in her head and her hair was wild around her face.

"Bonnie!"

At her voice, Bonnie snapped out of whatever trance she was in and she shivered. Her cheeks flushed and she apologized.

"I'm sorry. Here you are, love."

Hope had no idea what had happened to Bonnie in that moment, but other than looking like she'd just been loved thoroughly, she looked fine. Hope blushed, thinking about how she'd put that look on Bonnie's face before and then she remembered what she was supposed to be doing.

"Sorry," she whispered to Jimmy as she took the ring from the small, lace-covered pillow, and she took his left hand in hers.

"With this ring, I thee wed."

She slid the ring on his finger and before Lionel had a chance to pronounce them man and wife, Jimmy pulled her into his arms and kissed her deeply, and a bit inappropriately for church.

"Well," Lionel chuckled. "It seems my brother is in a hurry to claim his bride. "I pronounce you man and wife, and you may continue kissing the bride."

Hope smiled happily at Jimmy. "I love you," she whispered.

"You have made me the happiest man," Jimmy spoke against her lips before claiming them once more.

The congregation erupted in cheers and music played from some-where. Hope pulled back from the kiss and looked for Bonnie. She blew them a kiss and then hurried down the aisle toward Canneo and Danaá. They'd agreed to get the babies back to the guest rooms before the reception so they could be kept clear of the curious hands of the congregation.

Hope looked to Jimmy, who'd watched their family exit safely, and they smiled at each other.

"I can't wait to get you alone," he said, the corner of his lips turning up in a hungry smile.

"Me neither. Do we have to go to the reception?"

Jimmy laughed. "For the shortest possible amount of time," he said, leaning down to kiss her once more. He spoke next to her ear. "You didn't need to take the ring, my love. I don't want you wearing it after tonight."

Hope pushed up on her toes so she could speak in his ear. "Gladys explained that it would make things, um, more intense when we are joined. And that it would make you stronger. I want to give that to you." She hoped she'd done the right thing.

Jimmy stood straighter and Hope gasped when she saw his face. Green light flickered behind his pupils, and she saw the beginnings of the black lines under the skin of his throat. She knew what that meant, and it sent a jolt of lust straight to her core. She was going to make love to him properly tonight. It wouldn't be like the awful times with her deceased husband where he'd done everything in his power to make her feel awful and cause her excruciating pain. She knew from being intimate with Bonnie that when it was love, it was right, and it felt good.

She smiled at her husband. "The shortest reception in history. Then I want you to take me to bed, Mr. Manwaring." She used his taken name out of respect for his wish that he remain that man despite being surrounded by his brothers and the world he'd left behind. She would be Hope Manwaring from this day forward, her children would have the name Manwaring, and their lives would be intertwined forever.

His gaze grew even more heated, and she worried about the scene they were making in front of everyone who continued cheering them on. Jimmy bent down and slid his arm under her knees, picked her up and caused her to squeal. He turned to face his brother, who laughed heartily.

"We'll go on ahead. You two take your time."

Hope caught a glimpse of black lines on Lionel's face just before Jimmy turned her and walked swiftly back toward his brother's mansion. He climbed the stairs two at a time while Hope held on for dear life. When he arrived at their guest room on the third floor, which Gladys explained was the bridal suite, Jimmy shifted her so he could open the door, and then he carried her over the first of many thresholds he would as her husband. She laughed as he closed the door with his heel and then reached back with one hand to lock the door.

"Hold on," he said. His voice had deepened to that tone that sent a thrill through Hope.

She took a moment to glance around the room before he placed her on the bed. The dark wood on the walls would have seemed cold if not for the fire burning in the hearth and the candles lit around the room. Gladys had assured her the room would be a very special place for them to share their wedding night, and she'd delivered on that assurance.

"I know I'm supposed to share you with everyone tonight, but I can't—"

"Then don't," she said. Hope was just as eager to be alone.

Jimmy stood at the foot of the bed and hurriedly shed his coat and tailored shirt. His bare chest was so pale, but the black lines were more pronounced here. They throbbed in time with his heart beat. Hope crawled toward him and his breath caught. She traced lines with her fingers along the course of his veins. "Does it hurt?"

"No."

Hope smiled at him as she ran her hands down his chest to his belt. She unbuckled it and slid it so quickly from around his waist that it snapped through the loops. Jimmy gathered the hem of her dress and slid his hands slowly up her sides until his motion required her to lift her arms to be free of her clothes. She'd fed the babies shortly before dressing, so she felt safe going without a brassiere under the dress. Gladys had assured her the fit would be perfect, and she'd been right.

"Do these hurt?" Jimmy asked as he ran his hands tenderly along her swollen breasts.

"Tender, but not painful." She smiled.

Jimmy groaned as he bent to kiss her breasts and rub his face across them. He'd shaved recently, but there was still a pleasant burn from the friction.

Hope couldn't wait to finally see him bare before her. She slid her hands below the waist of his pants and leaned forward to kiss his chest. He felt so different than Bonnie. Where she was soft and pliant, his muscles were hard under skin dusted with coarse hairs across his chest. He smelled of aftershave and desire, so much so Hope felt drunk with the scent of him.

Jimmy slid a finger over her panties and his eyes flashed with green light.

"Do you hurt? From the delivery?"

"No."

She pulled at his pants, which were snug around his strong backside. Once they were past his hips they slid down his thick thighs to the floor. He wore plain white boxers which were pulled open in the front by his erection. For the first time Hope was nervous. She'd only ever been intimate with her husband before meeting Bonnie. What if it was always awful with a man? What if he hurt her?"

"Why do you tremble, my love?" Jimmy lifted her chin with his finger. "Do you fear me?"

"Not you. But this. Will it hurt?"

Jimmy pulled her gently into his arms, taking care not to hold her too tightly.

"I would never hurt you." His chest rose and fell as though he was breathing hard. "We don't have to—"

"Yes. We do. I want to. I'm just...It was so awful before."

Jimmy squeezed her tight and a pained sound came from him.

"I will do everything in my power to make this unbelievably

special for you, but if you would rather I just hold you in my arms, this never has to go any further. You are my wife whether or not we ever make love."

"Please, Jimmy. I want to try. I trust you."

Hope took a deep breath and slid her hands under the waistband of his boxers. She gasped as she slid them over his skin and the head of his cock appeared. It bounced against his stomach, standing so tall and proud, so truly a thing of beauty.

"Jimmy you are..."

"Let me love you," he said, his voice so powerful as it vibrated along her skin, sending shudders through her body. She lay back on the bed and opened herself for him, wanting nothing more than to be covered by his powerful body despite any lingering fear.

He knelt on the edge of the bed and crawled toward her, the green light from his eyes bathing her in light. She wanted his touch, craved it, needed him so close so deep. Her thoughts swirled into a mindless state of lust that could only be sated if he would just—

"*Oh,*" she cried as he began to worship her with his tongue. The insides of her thighs, the hollows of her pelvic bones, the skin marked from her pregnancy, he licked her everywhere before settling between her thighs and pleasuring her the way only Bonnie had before. It was a different sensation altogether but thrilling none-theless. His strong hands forced her body to comply to his will, and she found she didn't mind it one bit as he made her body reach highs she hadn't ever experienced before.

He gave her no chance to catch her breath before he kissed her deeply. She barely had the strength to hold on.

"My love, I don't want to hurt you," he growled. "But Hope, I—"

"Please, Jimmy. Please."

She wasn't sure what happened next. She felt an intense pressure that gave way to such pleasure she felt the earth move, literally. The room vibrated around them as wave after wave of energy passed through her body, bringing her and Jimmy closer and closer together until their bodies were as one and their ecstasy built and built until she couldn't breathe or see or speak.

Hope fought to open her eyes. She wanted to see, she wanted to watch. What she witnessed was like nothing she'd ever imagined.

Every muscle in Jimmy's body writhed under the surface of his flesh. His eyes glowed green and his skin crawled with the black lines, but it was the flames that frightened and thrilled her at the same time. Green fire burned all around them, unbearably hot and yet it added to her pleasure.

"Does it hurt?" she moaned.

"*No.*"

The windows rattled with the force of his voice. The force of their lovemaking slammed the bedframe into the wall. Her cries echoed around the room and spurred him on.

"I can't get close enough to you," Hope cried.

Jimmy pulled her onto his lap. She loved the way his cock slid into her as though it was meant to forever fill that part of her. At this angle she felt him so deep she thought for sure she would feel pain, but the pleasure was so incredible she clawed at his back to get closer. They kissed, but it was feral, animalistic. Teeth, nails, fingers, all used to gain leverage as the two attempted to be one.

"Jimmy," she cried as the flames consumed her. She came longer, harder, and more intense than before. Jimmy's fingers gripped the top of her shoulders, bringing her body down again and again until he threw back his head and shouted, the green flames shooting from his eyes and mouth. She felt a new heat inside her as he released, his seed lighting her up from the inside. Suddenly the window shattered and Jimmy threw up his arm to protect her from any flying glass. Then the bed shifted and a leg broke sending the two of them tumbling to the floor, laughing as they fell.

"Whatever will we tell your brother?" She fought to catch her breath, but between the outrageous exercise and the laughter, it was several minutes before she could breathe normally.

Jimmy held her close, caressing her skin wherever he could reach. "It serves him right," Jimmy said. "He wanted fire, he got one."

Hope turned her face to gaze at her husband. His hair had come uncombed and fell into his eyes. She brushed a lock from his forehead and loved that he was hers to touch like this. "What do you mean?"

"Why do you think Gladys had you wear the ring? I wish you hadn't, by the way. You must take it off," he said, reaching for her hand.

She pulled it back out of his reach. "But doesn't it make you stronger? Would any of this have happened?" She gestured to the wreckage that was their bridal suite and they laughed once more.

"I don't need the silver to react this way to you. You bring out the fire in me whether you're wearing it or not." He kissed her, caressing her cheek with his thumb. "In all seriousness, I want you to take it off. The silver acts as a conduit. If you are wearing it, my brothers may try to influence you, and I won't have that. You are *my* wife and I will protect you. I can't do that if you wear the tainted silver."

Hope slipped the ring off of her finger, immediately missing its weight. Jimmy must have noticed.

"Do not fret, my love. I have the perfect thing to replace it."

He sat up and reached for the pocket of his coat. He brought out a small velvet box and opened it for her. Inside sat an elegant silver-colored ring with three rows of what appeared to be diamonds.

"Jimmy! It's beautiful!"

He took it out and reached for her hand, sliding it effortlessly onto her left ring finger.

"It's white gold. I bought one for Bonnie as well. I don't know if she'll wear it..."

"Be patient with her," Hope said softly. "She cares for you."

He sighed and looked away. "I know that. And I understand why she refused, but I want her to know that she is important."

"She does."

Hope handed over the tainted silver ring but didn't release it right away.

"Maybe we should keep this for, you know, special occasions." She giggled and that was all it took for Jimmy to return to an amorous state. They made love on the floor in front of the fireplace this time. There were no more green flames, no broken furniture or glass, but Hope felt just as close to her new husband.

HOURS later they returned to their guest room so Hope could feed the babies. Bonnie slept soundly in the bed, but Canneo and Danaá stood close by, guarding the infants. Jimmy changed little man's diaper while Hope fed girlie and then they switched. Hope had missed them being away for a few short hours, but she hadn't been worried. She knew Bonnie and the men would care for them.

Once they were situated, Hope and Jimmy returned to the bridal suite and spent the remainder of the night talking, laughing, and kissing under the moonlight that shone through the broken window.

"I suppose I'll have to pay for that," Jimmy said with an exaggerated sigh. The fire was warm enough that the bitter cold winds didn't affect their comfort.

"I suppose." Hope turned to face him. "So what happens now? Will your brothers let us be to raise our family? Will we be safe?"

"That remains to be seen. With William away these past weeks and Nathaniel not yet home, I don't know what will happen when they return. Nathaniel and I were very close, once. I don't know what our reunion will be like. William, on the other hand, we never got along. He enjoyed bullying me as a child, and as a grown man he resented me for having my own mind. I'm sure sparks will fly between us, but he's always listened to Lionel, and if Lionel and I have an agreement, perhaps we will find a truce."

"I sure hope so. I'd very much like for us to have some peace in our lives, especially for the babies."

Jimmy kissed her temple as he held her closer. Loving his new wife and their companion was almost enough to convince him that perhaps he could be absolved of all that had happened to this point.

"I pray you are right."

19

Two weeks later...

Bonnie enjoyed coming down to the bar to listen to Jimmy play the piano late in the evening. She and Hope would sometimes come together, but tonight Hope remained behind with Byron and his fussy self and Bonnie needed to get out. She wanted a drink and knew that Jimmy had found a steady supplier for the hotel's bar. It made the Inn at Lake's Crossing a popular destination.

She sat at the far end of the bar from the piano in the shadows watching their patrons dance, drink, and laugh the night away. She felt somewhat content in their new life here in Reno, happy with Jimmy and Hope and the babies, bored some of the time, and a bit restless to be honest.

She hadn't forgotten either what happened the night of the wedding. Neither had the guests of Lionel Bane's compound. Some thought they'd had a freak storm of some kind, but Bonnie knew from speaking to Gladys exactly what had happened when her companions joined in holy matrimony.

There had been that moment during the ceremony when Jimmy placed the tainted silver ring on Hope's finger. Bonnie had been blasted with heat, as though she'd stood too near a fire, and it burned her from the inside out. It had been agonizing—yet rapturous—and she'd lost a few moments there. When she came to, it appeared only Hope, Jimmy, and Lionel had been affected, but that may not have been the case. Gladys spoke to her on the walk to the reception, which Hope and Jimmy missed completely, and she'd hinted at the rush she'd felt during the ceremony. Bonnie had laughed it off, but there was definitely something to what she'd said. Everyone in the place had seemed more amorous that night, and then later when several windows in the gathering hall had shattered and a pulse of energy had followed, going straight to her womb, Bonnie knew that all she'd heard about this evil silver hadn't been the full story. There was something even stronger at work here and she intended to find out.

"You seem deep in thought, miss. May I sit with you?"

Bonnie wasn't quite sure how she'd missed him. The man was massive. He hulked over her, blocking her completely from view. She knew she could reach out to Jimmy, or even Canneo and Danaá as they'd devised a way to communicate in order to keep the children safe, but she wanted to hear this man out.

"You must be William." Her smile was arrogant. She wanted him to know that she was no flimsy dame. She could hold her own with the likes of the Bane brothers. Jimmy had made sure of that.

"And you are a lovely woman, Miss Collins. I apologize that I am only just returning to town. I hate that I've missed seeing your pretty face these past weeks. My brother assures me that of the two companions my youngest sibling returned to Reno with, you were the prettier of the two."

Bonnie's gaze turned cold. Ah. So William was a bigot. Or an idiot. Either way, she planned to use the situation to her advantage.

"And what kept you away? I understand you have quite the silver-smith business here in town, among other diversions." She'd heard he ran a brothel on the outskirts of town, that he made quite a bit of money pouring bootlegged liquor into those trying to drown their sorrows while indulging in the flesh. There were many who were looking for an escape as the rest of the country was plunged into the worst economic crisis many had seen in their lifetimes or longer. Jimmy had assured her they were fine, that he'd diversified his holdings over the past fifty years, but she knew even he was nervous about the desperate state. More and more he wanted Bonnie and Hope to remain in their penthouse atop the Inn so he didn't have to worry about their well-being, with miscreants and other troublemakers that had found their way to Reno.

William's gaze roamed Bonnie's body, leaving heat wherever it landed. Unlike when Jimmy looked at her with love, this heat felt dirty. "I have made quite a nice fortune over the past several lifetimes, it is true, but my first and foremost duty is to Lionel and the purpose all four Bane brothers were brought here to complete."

Bonnie shifted on her barstool. "So, what do you want, William? I've finished my drink and need a good reason to stay and speak to you." She figured appearing disinterested might keep him talking.

"I want to know, Miss Collins, what it would take to woo you. What would it take to lure you away from my brother? For a night, or forever?"

Bonnie bit back a laugh. He was so barking up the wrong tree. He had nothing she physically desired. And yet, she was entertaining his bargain, if only to learn more about this silver. Jimmy had forbidden her and Hope from wearing any of it, and though she didn't want to be influenced or manipulated in any way by the elder Banes, she wanted what they had.

Getting just a taste of the power from the silver on top of all she'd learned from Canneo and Danaá, she was beginning to desire more than her happy domestic bliss. She wanted to see just how powerful she could become as a witch. She knew there had been many in her family over the years, and she'd already been given a taste of what she might be able to be on her own. Would it be worth it to lay with this devil for some knowledge, some power of her own?

"Your offer is tempting. I'll get back to you on that, William."

She stood from her chair and slung her wrap over her shoulders. Her slim-fitting black dress hugged her curves and plunged low enough in the neckline that she knew every man, and a few of the women, desired her. William was no different. He murmured his approval as she turned her back on him.

"When will we meet again?" he asked, a twinge of that other-worldly tone Jimmy was known to get when seeking carnal affections could be heard in William's voice.

She looked back over her shoulder. "I'll find you."

20

Present Day
Fort Bragg, California

Byron stood by his jeep at four o'clock sharp, anxious to see Darcy again. He'd driven around all day getting the lay of the land here and working on a list of questions for Jonah:

1. What exactly is your involvement with my family?
2. How is that you look so young and yet you were the one who cheated my family out of their business?
3. How much of that story you told me is true?

Because Byron couldn't get over the wild tales the not-so-old man told him, foggy though he'd been about their discussion. As the day had gone on, however, he'd remembered more and more. Tainted silver? Special powers? It all seemed like bullshit to him, but something about it all seemed to resonate. He wanted to know more. He wanted to know his true family history, and something told him this Bane guy could fill in some of the blanks. Like what happened to the grandfather he was named for? And his twin sister? And why the men never stuck around in his family? He was determined to be different, and yet up until now he'd fucked up enough for a lifetime.

Coming to Fort Bragg felt like a new beginning, however. A chance to make a change. And if that change involved the lovely Darcy, well, who was he to complain?

At that moment, the open signed was flipped to closed and the door opened. Darcy breezed out her black pigtails blowing in the wind. She bent to retie the laces on one of her boots and showed so much thigh under her short skirt that Byron nearly dislocated his jaw with his reaction.

She's doing this on purpose to throw you off. Don't be fooled.

"Shut up," Byron said to his inner smart voice. So what if he wanted to let his innate biological urge to mate rule his thoughts every once in a while? He was entitled, wasn't he?

Darcy turned to him with a knowing smile, and it dawned on him that she'd just witnessed his internal battle firsthand and was hellbent on making him pay.

Oh, you'll pay.

"You ready to see the goods?" she asked, her tongue poking out the corner of her mouth as she smirked at him.

Answer her, dumbass!

Byron shook his head. "The silver, you mean? Yeah, yeah I'm good. Let's go see what you can do with your hands."

Oh, fuck me, you're a loser.

He really was, but he couldn't help himself around her. She was everything a guy like him wasn't supposed to want: gorgeous, intelligent, *white*.

Shit. Great-grandma Hope married a white man, and he took

damn good care of her until she died. It's not like Byron was looking for a wife here or anything, it was just...Darcy was the first girl he'd wanted to talk to since he'd returned home from the military. He'd been avoiding real life until now, and he was ready to dip his toe back in and see if he was ready.

You'll never be ready for a girl like her.

"Hey, you alright, Byron? You want to go grab some dinner before we go to my workshop?"

That might actually be a really good idea. Byron needed to cool his jets a bit.

"Yeah. My treat. You can tell me a little more about this place and that Bane guy."

Darcy laughed as he joined her on the sidewalk. "We'll need more than dinner for me to tell you about 'that Bane guy.' You like pizza?"

Byron chuckled. "Does anyone *not* like pizza?"

"Sure. Folks who are gluten or dairy-free. Vegans."

"Right. I'm none of those. I love pizza."

"Great. There's a place a couple of blocks up with great pizza and then I'll buy you a drink at the Golden West Saloon. You'll be very interested in that place."

Byron stopped walking as a jolt hit him in the chest. *What was that?*

"Why would I be interested in that place?"

Darcy turned around and smiled at him. "You have questions. I have answers. Let's go learn about your history."

Byron stood there, dazed. *How did she do that?*

Impatient, she held out her hand. "Are you coming?"

Byron knew that if he reached out and took her hand, his whole life would be thrown off its axis. Whatever knowledge she had hidden behind that coy smile was something he needed, but something that would change his life forever.

After a few beats Byron reached for her hand. Darcy's skin was soft and warm and immediately put him in a state of bliss. She could have suggested he jump off the cliffs near Glass Beach and he would have gladly complied.

"Come on, Byron Manwaring. I've got a story for you."

JONAH BANE WATCHED the two of them walk down the street hand in hand from the balcony off of the ballroom, and a little bit of his cold heart began to thaw. Maybe it was time for him to finally put an end to the Bane legacy, and Byron and Darcy were the right ones to help him. He was so tired and alone. He missed the loves of his life every day and was sick of hiding away in his tower of solitude. Perhaps if he told Byron everything, he and Darcy could be the ones to help him.

Jonah sensed movement near the front of the house and heard the chime alerting him that the front door had been opened and closed. He'd given his staff the rest of the week off. They had no guests scheduled, and he figured if he was really going to go through with his plan, he'd need to keep the house empty. Then who had arrived?

Jonah descended the steps and heard movement on the stairs below coming toward him. He stepped onto the landing of the second floor just as she reached the top. Her red hair flowed around her shoulders and her green eyes sparkled mischievously.

"Well hey there, Jimmy."

For the second time a bit of the cold in his chest seemed to crack and melt. Seeing this woman brought him so many memories, so many feelings, some good, some horrible. But there was no one else he'd rather have by his side at the moment he decided to take the path that would end over a century of grief.

"Hello, Bonnie. Am I glad to see you."

TO BE CONTINUED...
Stay Tuned for more...

AFTERWORD AND COMING NEXT
FROM R.L. MERRILL

The Banes of Lake's Crossing is a shared world created by Ellay Brandon, Kimberlie L. Faye, and R.L. Merrill. Future installments by all three authors are in the works.

If you love supernatural suspense and paranormal romance, check out The Gifted series by R.L. Merrill, or read on for an excerpt of her upcoming M/M vampire tale, which is linked to the Gifted series.

This is *Sundowners...*

Prologue
January 2018

Donna Hicks smoothed the fine silk skirt she'd picked out for her husband's event and fidgeted in the front seat of their McLaren. "Are you sure we're dressed all right?" She gave her husband's attire a onceover, grinning at how well the Hugo Boss hugged his lines.

"Of course, darling. You look stunning," her husband Timothy said, taking her hand and kissing the back of it. "Grant assured me that casual-nice was the dress code. Oh, honey, this is huge. I thought we'd have to wait at least a year before getting this invitation."

The McLaren handled the curves of Highway 17 with ease on the dark January night. They took a blind turn onto a two-lane road and then another onto a much narrower one with no street signs. Donna wasn't sure how Timothy knew where he was going, it was pitch black outside. The private drive was only wide enough for one car. Thankfully it was paved. Timothy had already had to take the new car into the shop because he'd run over a concrete parking barrier in the lot at the gym, scraping the underside of the luxury car.

"So tell me more about this group," she asked her husband of sixteen years. "Am I allowed to discuss my research or should I simply play the trophy wife tonight?"

Timothy chuckled. "They know about your work," he said. "I brag about you all the time. Just be yourself. They invited us because we meet their requirements for membership, I guess." He laughed nervously. "I just didn't think it would happen so soon."

"Timothy, you made your company over a billion dollars last quarter. You've revitalized the processes for your team and you've already been promoted twice despite only being there for a year. I think you've shown these people that you are absolutely worth their investment."

When Timothy had told Donna about the opportunity to join a private club for influential Silicon Valley business people, she'd been intrigued. He hadn't had a lot of details, but he'd been so excited. She'd grown up on the Peninsula, but he'd been raised in the Central Valley, and had spent his career in finance trying to make people forget he was the son of farmers. They'd met when his original company invested in her medical research program and he'd checked all the boxes on her suitable-husband-qualities list. He was younger than her, independently wealthy, no children and didn't care to have them, and more than happy to let her rule the roost in their Palo Alto mansion.

"Here we are," he said, and they both took a moment to breathe.

The magnificent structure before them was all glass, redwood, and steel. It was illuminated from within with soft lighting that only went as far as the thick copse of trees surrounding the house. The roof appeared to be...moving?

"It's got a green roof even," Timothy breathed. "It's just like the Meta offices. I bet you can't even tell there's a home here from above." He parked between a Ferrari and a custom Tesla and shut off the engine. "I can't believe we're here."

"Timothy, just promise me one thing?"

"Anything, darling," he said, taking her hands in his. "I want you to be comfortable with this too."

With great wealth comes great opportunities.

"Let's not get in over our heads, you know what I mean? If they start asking for us to commit money or time...talk to me before you make any decisions? We've worked really hard to pay off the houses and cars. I want us to have something to show for the sacrifices we've made."

"Absolutely," he said, but she knew he'd probably forget the moment they were inside. "I want us to have all the things we've dreamed of. A long, happy, and healthy life together."

He pulled her forward and their lips met. He really was a sweet man. Hardworking, decent. Took good care of his body, and took excellent care of her in bed. They were a team, and if all they'd heard about the private club Elite Ventures Enterprises was true, they were going to be a part of something important.

"Let's do this," she said, kissing him once more. He pulled back and growled a little before moving back in for a deeper kiss. She laughed as he slid a hand under her skirt.

"There will be time for that later," she purred. "All you want."

They left the car and climbed the steps up to the front door, which opened as they approached. Timothy took her hand and smiled at the tuxedoed man at the door.

"Mr. and Mrs. Timothy Hicks," the man said as he gestured with his hand. They stepped inside and the door closed behind them with a whoosh. Donna's heels clicked loudly on the concrete floor. The foyer was wide and empty save for a few sculptures and paintings. Two tall vases stood on either side of an interior doorway before them that was completely dark. Timothy hesitated and the man from the door called out, "Please, step inside."

Donna felt Timothy squeeze her hand, and then they stepped into the darkness, ready to take their lives to the next level. For a split second before her heel connected with the floor, she thought perhaps they were pushing their luck, that they'd already been so fortunate. Was joining the organization more than they deserved?

The darkness enveloped them, and with it, Donna felt hands on her arms and shoulders. Timothy's hand was pulled from hers and replaced with a stranger's. Bodies pressed against her and she tried to fight the panic. She whispered her husband's name but only heard muffled voices around her, attempting to sooth her, quiet her. Prepare her.

The light came on—and she gasped at what she saw.

It was too late to turn back now. She knew that, and yet she dug her heels in, afraid to move any closer. She'd lost sight of Timothy and was now on her own, and yet she wasn't alone. More bodies closed in on her, like people crowding a full elevator heading to the lobby at the end of a long workweek, everyone excited for the weekend.

And just like in an elevator, the floor began to lower.

"Welcome, guests." The voice that came over the loudspeaker reminded Donna of something out of a sci-fi movie. "The Source is grateful for your work and dedication. Please prepare to pay tribute, and then we shall begin your introduction."

Donna sucked in a breath and before she could exhale, the press of bodies came even closer. She felt like screaming, and then she was bathed in a warm light from above, until everything was...fine.

She sighed, letting her body go slack, and heard sounds of approval around her. Everything was glorious, everything was wonderful. She'd never felt better...

Chapter One
    Creed

January 2019

"Well, Mr. Lowell, I think we have everything we need. Your references all check out, and you passed your background check. Can you start on Friday?"

What a relief! I smiled and leaned against the wall of my dingy hotel room. *Thank goodness for excellent references.* I inhaled the combination mildew/chlorine smell caused by the permanent dampness from the ocean and the indoor swimming pool below my room, and felt gratitude knowing I wouldn't be in this hotel much longer. This was the break I needed, or my current accommodations would soon go from bad to worse.

"Thank you, yes. What time does the evening shift start?" I kept my fingers crossed while I waited for the answer.

"Six o'clock. Just come to the front desk and our evening supervisor will get you set up. Lexi's great. She'll show you the ropes."

"Wonderful. Thank you for this opportunity."

"We should be thanking *you*, Mr. Lowell. You're overqualified for the position, and we've had a difficult time keeping our evening staff. I hope this works out for the both of us."

I thanked Yvonne, the Human Resources director, once more before disconnecting. Then the victory dance commenced.

"Did you hear that, Rhonda? We're in!"

My red Doberman rested her jaw on her paws and made an old lady noise, indicating that she'd rather be napping than dancing.

I would not be thwarted, however. I danced a *West Side Story* routine across the room to the kitchenette and reached into the fridge with panache. There was one last bag of A-positive that I'd been sipping on since arriving in Santa Cruz, and now I could finish it off since I'd have a steady supply in just two days' time. Not that I needed much—especially not when I was working—but it was important to never let my energy stores deplete. It affected my judgement and my ability to do the work that was so desperately needed.

I did a spin and a box step before kicking my leg out and throwing my arms back in a layout. Sunset was the time of day I experienced a massive surge of energy. I was at my most powerful, and able to do the most good for my patients, as the sun made its descent in the West. I loved being back on the coast, close to the healing waters of the Pacific and the place where I'd gained my enhanced existence. I shivered as I moved about my cramped space, loving the ripple of the power flowing through my limbs. It had been a while since I'd been able to use the energy to help my patients, so I needed to work it out a bit on my own, and dancing made my heart happy.

Hopefully I'd find someone who knew the old dances at Puesta Del Sol, my new place of employment. The patients who loved to dance and sing with me were the most fun to work with, but honestly, I loved them all. By helping them, I received strength in return. It was the perfect arrangement.

It wouldn't take long to pack my things. My lone duffel bag contained seven sets of scrubs, a suit, three white t-shirts, a pair of jeans, a Harvard hoodie, two pairs of shoes, and a small photo album that contained cherished pictures of my parents and younger siblings. The rest of my belongings and resources were hidden in pre-paid storage facilities around the country for when I got desperate... or had to run.

My family was all gone now. My little sister was my last living relative, and she'd passed away four months ago according to the hometown newspaper in Macon County, Georgia. I read every copy that I could get ahold of through the local libraries. The internet had been such a great invention. Even though I hadn't been home in nearly forty years, I'd managed to keep tabs on everyone. They'd all lived mostly happy, satisfying lives and died of natural causes at advanced ages, which was the best I could have hoped for.

But now that I had no worry of repercussions for my family, I could finally seek out the truth.

Puesta Del Sol was hopefully the end of the line. The last

assisted-living home where I'd worked in Albuquerque had led me here, to Santa Cruz, California. "Go west, young man," turned out to be the advice I'd needed all along.

I was determined to find those responsible for sending me on this decades-long exile. It wouldn't be long now. It was time to set things straight, and it seemed fitting to be back near where it all started.

ACKNOWLEDGMENTS

Thank you Ellay and Kimberlie for creating and sharing this world with me. I can't wait until we can all visit the Banes together again.

Thank you to Kelli Collins for her editing expertise and assistance in keeping the world on track for us.

To Amber from Writing Diversely for helping me ensure that I treated my characters' identities with respect and love in this story.

To J. Scott Coatsworth for giving me the kick in the pants I needed to finally release this story. You didn't know that's what you did, but you did, but you did, and I thank you. You are such a huge support to our queer writing community and I'm grateful you are in my authory world.

And to the Roadies and all of my readers who kept the love of the Banes alive. I hope you love this latest installment!

ABOUT R.L. MERRILL

Whether she's writing contemporary romance featuring quirky and relatable characters or diving deep into the paranormal and super-natural to give readers a shiver, R.L. Merrill loves creating compelling stories that will stay with readers long after. Winner of the Kathryn Hayes "When Sparks Fly" Best Contemporary award for *Hurricane Reese*, and a Foreword INDIES finalist for *Summer of Hush*, Ro spends every spare moment improving her writing craft and striving to find that perfect balance between real-life and happily ever after. She writes diverse and inclusive romance, contributes paranormal hilarity to Robyn Peterman's Magic and Mayhem Universe, and pens horror-inspired music reviews for HorrorAddicts.net. You can find her connecting with readers on social media, advocating for America's youth, raising two brilliant kids, or headbanging at a rock show near her home in the San Francisco Bay Area! *Stay Tuned for more...*

Sign up for her newsletter-y thingie at www.rlmerrillauthor.com

facebook.com/rlmerrillauthor

twitter.com/rlmerrillauthor

instagram.com/rlmerrillauthor

amazon.com/R-L-Merrill/e/B00PI6Q1LI

ALSO BY R.L. MERRILL

Haunted Series: (Contemporary Romance)

Haunted

Fated

Bated

Jaded – (Coming Soon)

Minded Series: (Paranormal Spinoff of Haunted Series)

Minded

Blossomed

Father F'in' Christmas

A Peculiar Prom Night

Magic and Mayhem Universe: (Funny Paranormal Romance in the universe created by Robyn Peterman)

Shifted

Ghoul Me Once

Gator Me Twice

Magic and Mayhem/Shifted Collection

Fang Me Three Times

Fangtastic Four

Next Installment October 2022

Hollywood Rock 'n' Romance Trilogy: (Contemporary Romance)

Teacher

Teacher: Act Two

Teacher: The Final Act

Contemporary Romance Series:

The Rock Season

Road Trip

You Fell First

The Heart Knows (Re-Release 2022)

A Match Made in Spain

LGBTQ Romance

Pinups and Puppies (Originally in Love Is All Vol. 2)

I Want, More – Bolder Breed Studios #1 (Love Is All Vol. 3)

Love and Pride – Bolder Breed Studios #2 (Love Is All Vol. 4, out solo November 2021)

The Banes of Lake's Crossing (Historical Horror Romance)

The Fourth Man (The Banes of Lake's Crossing) (Historical Horror Romance)

The Redemption of Nathaniel Bane

The Absolution of Jonah Bane

The Banes of Lake's Crossing - Ascension (Coming Soon)

The Gifted Series: (Supernatural Suspense/Paranormal Romance)

Healer

Connection

Sundowners (M/M Paranormal Romance

Sundowners Book One – (September 2022)

Forces of Nature Series: (Gay Contemporary Romance)

Hurricane Reese

Typhoon Toby

Earthquake Ethan (Coming Soon)

Summer of Hush Series: (Gay Contemporary Romance)

Summer of Hush

Brains and Brawn

Book Three (Coming Soon)

HEA Collective – A Patreon-Exclusive Series featuring Award-Winning and Bestselling Authors writing trope-based diverse and inclusive romance stories. Details coming soon.

March 2023

June 2023

Anthologies:

Thanksgiving Day Parade From Hell (Worst Holiday Ever) (Gay Contemporary Romance

Valentine's Day From Hell (Worst Valentine's Day Ever) (Gay Contemporary Romance)

Salty and Sweet (Summer Fair) (Lesbian Contemporary Romance)

A Piece of Him (Gone With The Dead) (Horror)

Breaking Bread—Dark Divinations from HorrorAddicts.net Press (Horror)

Exchange (QSF Flash Fiction Anthology - Renewal) (Science Fiction)

Tap-Tap-Tap (QSF Flash Fiction Anthology - Impact) (Horror)

Human Sacrifice (QSF Flash Fiction Anthology - Innovation) (Horror)

Joy Is A Phone Call Away – A More Perfect Union (Lesbian Contemporary Romance)

The House Must Fall – Haunts and Hellions from HorrorAddicts.net Press – May 2021 (Horror)

A Kept Woman – BAQWA Presents: Horror Show 2021(Lesbian Horror Romance)

Gods of Rock 'n' Roll (email Ro for a copy at rlmerrillauthor@gmail.com)

How Bittersweet is Karma?

Let Me Stand Next To Your Fire (Love Is All Vol. 5 — Out June 14, 2022)

Holiday Romance

A Peace Offering (Re-release)

Love and Pride – Bolder Breed Studios #2

Audiobooks

The Rock Season (Kiss App)

Brains and Brawn (Kiss App)

Teacher (Kiss App)

Hurricane Reese (Kiss App)

A Match Made in Spain (Summer 2022)

Healer: Gifted Book One (Summer 2022)

Non-Fiction

Horror Addicts Guide To Life Volume 2 - Edited by Emerian Rich

Death's Garden Revisited - Edited by Loren Rhoads (Out Fall 2022)

www.ingramcontent.com/pod-product-compliance
Lightning Source LLC
Chambersburg PA
CBHW032210170626
46808CB00006B/2409